Running From Darkness

Book 3 Dark River Stone Collective

JP Sayle

Copyright

Book Formatting by JP Sayle
Proofreading Virginie

Warning
Some of the content of this book is sexually graphic, with the use of explicit language and adult situations involving two males. It is only intended for mature audiences.
Trigger Warnings
There are scenes of rape depicted (not of the two main characters but a side character) in this book. If this is a trigger, then this is possibly not the book to read.

Conall is on the run. Kyle wants someone who will want him for who he is. Can they find what they need in each other, or will it all blow up in their faces?

An unthinkable situation leads Conall to violence. On the run with his injured sister, he makes a snap decision to seek the favor that the Dark Angels' president, Killer, owes the Chosen Few. When Conall's brothers turn their back on him, he has everything to lose if Killer refuses to help. When Kyle, a member of the Dark Angels, gives him a place to stay, Conall realizes the most valuable thing he could lose isn't his freedom but his heart.

Kyle is in a dating funk. Then late one night, while caring for Killer's daughter, River, a late-night visitor throws him a curveball. As everything unravels, Kyle offers Conall sanctuary in his home. But will Conall's past make it impossible for there to be more between them? Kyle's putting everything on the line, but is Conall?

Running from Darkness, the third book in Dark River Stone Collective, is an MC gay romance with angst, hurt-comfort, and newfound family.

Dedication

To Sam & JJ who tirelessly worked to get me to write the words and bring the third book in this series to life!

Contents

Prologue

Kyle

"What's your plan for the evening?" Mom called from the kitchen as I lounged on the couch, flicking through my message thread with Nutty, Troy, and Ali. We all worked for the same tattoo shop in Belton.

At the sound of dishes clinking together, I got from the couch, pushed my cell phone into my back pocket, and headed into the kitchen to help wash dishes. The shiny new dishwasher sat next to the sink, untouched. Dad bought the gift last year for Christmas. It hadn't gone down too well, hence why it remained unused. Mom could hold a grudge for a very long time. Her argument was simple. Who got a loved one a house appliance as a gift?

The cozy kitchen smelled like home: baked bread and cookies. The table where I'd sat as a child doing homework under her watchful eye bore scratches, yet she wouldn't part with it. The curtains, which she changed every six months, were currently red with white flowers. I missed these constants when I was back in Belton.

Picking up the dishcloth, I walked to the counter, grabbed one of the wet plates, and dried it.

She glanced sideways and aimed a bright smile in my direction. "Always the helpful one. I bet your brother has disappeared up to his bedroom."

Jackson had moved back home six weeks earlier after splitting up with his girlfriend, and he was back in his old bedroom for the foreseeable future. "He's got a hot date with... shit, I forget, but it ain't the same one from two days ago."

"That boy is always looking for a sweeter pot of honey. He'll learn one day that he has to fill the pot himself if he wants to keep things sweet."

Bubbles of laughter erupted out of me. Mom was always coming up with some analogy or another. "I'm gonna have to remember that one."

Her blonde curls bounced as she shook her head. "You were never one to dip your wick into every boy you liked. You've always wanted more from a relationship."

"Mom, seriously! Ick, that's gross." Although I didn't argue with her, not when I was planning on meeting my best friend from school, Ink, because he had someone he thought I might be interested in getting to know in the biblical sense.

"It's not like I don't know what you get up to." My eyes widened in horror at the idea, and I was glad she changed the subject before I had to. "You never said if you're going out tonight? You seem to have spent nearly all your vacation hanging around the house."

Placing the dry plate on the counter, I picked up the next one. "Hey, you saying you don't want me here?" I added affront to my voice, holding back the grin.

A dripping, soapy finger pointed in my direction. "Stop being an idiot. You're normally more social when you're home, that's all."

I aimed a genuine smile at her to show I was fine. I'd come home for some downtime. "Was thinking of meeting Ink at Shorty's. There's a band playing tonight, and he's been pestering me since I got home to catch up." I didn't add the possible hookup. Again, she did not need to know about that, or that it had been forever since I'd gotten a particular itch scratched. I'd let Ink persuade me to meet the guy he'd been talking up. "We're slammed at work, and Linc has had a few issues he's needed to work through."

My family was aware I was a patched member of Dark Angels. They chose not to discuss what that meant, and if I was honest, I preferred not to talk about stuff that would worry them. I classed Linc and his daughter, River, as extended family, along with the members of Dark Angels. A fucked-up bitch had set Linc up and left him currently wading through a shit storm. None of which I could help with.

"You could always come home and go into business with Ink. He's doin' real well, I hear."

It was a refrain I'd heard before. And as much as I loved Ink and my family, working in Linc's tattoo shop pushed me to be a better artist. Linc was a phenomenal tattoo artist. A six-month waiting list to get an appointment spoke to the man and his talent. Irrespective of the fact he was president of Dark Angels, he encouraged others to find their potential. I'd grown as an artist, and he challenged me to expand my skills. He didn't box me in, and it was why I'd never leave to come home. "Ma, you know I love working for Linc. He took me on when I was just starting out, and I get a lot out of working alongside him. He's got a lot to teach me."

"You're an amazing artist in your own right."

Before she could launch into the wasting talent speech, I slung my arm over her shoulders, giving her a half-hug. "I know, and I get to use that talent every day doing tattoos. Living pieces of artwork. A human canvas. There is no better way to honor what I love, Mom." I kissed her cheek to take the sting out of my words. I understood she wanted me close by, but Ink, though a great tattooist, had no desire to push himself, which was fine for him.

"I worry," she said as she turned toward me. "And it would be great to have both my boys back under my roof."

I hugged her a little closer and gave her a toothy grin. "You got a short memory, Mom. How many times did you complain about our bickerin' at each other?"

She giggled, sounding young and carefree. "You got me there. The way you two were, I should be completely gray by now."

Squinting at her head. "I think a see a few silver ones."

She slapped my arm with her soapy hand, wetting my favorite band T-shirt. "Hey. How am I gonna wear this out tonight?"

"Hay is for horses," she fired back like she'd done ever since I could remember. "And there's a dryer not ten feet from you." She went back to washing the pots, and the back-and-forth banter continued till we were done.

Thirty minutes later, I was heading out the door with my T-shirt a little more wrinkled but dry. I hadn't bothered to change since Ink wouldn't care what I had on with my Levi's.

Shorty's was a familiar hangout for folks that liked rock and were more gay than straight. It was where I'd met my first boyfriend. I'd been a late bloomer in figuring shit out. Ink and I had hung out here as far back as I could remember.

Swinging the door open, the blast of sound nearly deafened me, and the heat and scent of liquor were heady. The band on the stage was going hard, making it difficult to tell whether they were talented. I edged past several men to reach where I knew Ink preferred to stand. The spot was at the end of the bar, out of the way of foot traffic.

I lifted my hand to wave when his dark head moved away from the preppy-looking guy and he glanced in my direction after the dude nudged his shoulder. It would seem Ink had shown the guy my picture. From the curl of his lip after his gaze swept over me, he wasn't impressed. I dialed up the smile I aimed at him by several notches. It stung to potentially get rejected before he'd even spoken to me. What was his deal?

Seeing this could head south pretty quickly, but not giving up just yet, I shouted to be heard over the din and pointed at the half-empty beer bottles in front of them. "Want a beer?"

Both men nodded, and I swung my gaze to the busy staff behind the bar. I held up my twenty and waited my turn, watching the dude with Ink from the corner of my eye. He was cute, if not a little clean-cut for my tastes. His eyes were a delicate blue, and though his chin looked weak, I could see the potential.

Once I had the beers, I moved closer just in time to hear the dude say, "He's so scruffy. What did he do, sleep in his T-shirt?"

Ink didn't answer as he gave me an apologetic smile. It took effort to keep my own in place. "Nah, Mom soaked it messin' around, so she put it in the dryer about twenty minutes ago." I pointed at the creases from the high heat. "It got a little wrinkled, and I ran out of time to do anything about it. I thought it would be rude to show up late. Hi, I'm Kyle." I placed the beers on the bar and offered him my hand, working on being friendly.

He eyed it for a long second before taking it. "Flynn." He clasped my hand for the briefest of handshakes. Not that I'd call it a handshake, more a limp-wrist wriggle motion that was over before it started.

I shrugged off the weirdness of the moment and gave Ink a wide grin. "Hey, squirt."

Red crept past the neck of Flynn's pressed button-down as he snatched up his beer and took a drink, looking away. No apology for being rude was forthcoming.

Ink nudged my shoulder. "One time I squirted you with ink, and you ain't never gonna let me live it down."

Around the laughter, I shook my head. "Nope. It's good to see ya, man. You're looking good." And he was. Someone had cut his dark hair since the last time I'd seen him. The layered cut highlighted his slashing cheekbones and hazel eyes. I picked up my bottle and pointed it at his neck. "You got a new tat. Who did it for you?"

Preppy Boy made a huffing sound, and I wondered why Ink had suggested I might be interested. He clearly wasn't. And I was still smarting from the scruffy comment. It wasn't like Ink and I dressed differently. We both liked band T-shirts and jeans, which made up most of my wardrobe. Was this why I wasn't getting laid?

"Got a new trainee in the shop, and she's got killer skills. You should pop by tomorrow before you head back to Belton so I can introduce you to her." He carried on chatting and catching me up.

I made a concentrated effort not to be rude and act like I was interested in Flynn, but in my head, I was counting down the minutes until I could leave.

On my way to the restroom for a much-needed break from acting like a grinning fool, a large guy stepped into my path. The way he moved was all bad-boy swagger, something I'd seen a lot of in Dark Angels. Was he a biker? He wasn't wearing any leather, but I got the sense he wouldn't look out of place in it. He was the type of guy who got my blood heating.

He glanced over my shoulder to where I'd left Ink and Flynn. One brow quirked up, and his massive shoulders moved, his thick biceps flexing in the well-fitting T-shirt. Was that disappointment I saw in his eyes?

Keeping it friendly, I smiled lazily. "Problem?"

Something about him seemed familiar when his gaze met mine. Yet, the eyes that would not easily be forgotten held my attention. The green was ringed with gray and held something similar to Linc's, a weight from living a hard life. It left its mark and compelled me to look closer. He smelled of soap and musk. The combination did something for me that Preppy Boy's expensive cologne hadn't. Desire unfurled in the pit of my stomach as he held my gaze, unblinking. My heart bounded as time ticked by unnoticed.

When someone knocked against my side, it broke the spell. As I glanced toward the apologetic guy stumbling off, it gave the dude I'd been having an eye-fucking competition with a chance to turn and walk into the crowd. My gaze dipped to his ass, and I shook my head.

When I lost sight of him, I released a shuddery breath. What the fuck was that? I rubbed the center of my chest, feeling my heart battering against my hand.

In the restroom, I stared at myself in the mirror. The flush and excited light in my eyes had fuck-all to do with Flynn and everything to do with the silent encounter.

After peeing, I walked back into the bar, intent on searching out the other guy. Ten minutes later, after coming up empty, I sighed heavily and trudged back to Ink. One look at Flynn's stony expression, and I figured it was time to leave.

I was out the door of Shorty's five minutes later, with a plan to go to Ink's the next day before heading back to Belton. I inhaled the fresh air, thinking about soap and musk. I walked toward home, the memory of a pair of green-gray eyes accompanying me.

Big fucking hairy balls!

Why couldn't Ink have introduced me to tall, dark, and mysterious?

Dating fucking sucked!

Chapter One

Conall

My cell phone distracted me from the fucked-up punch line of Gearhead's joke. Dropping the beer bottle I held onto the table, I dug into my jeans pocket for my phone. One look at the screen and my brows drew together.

"Gimme five," I muttered to Gearhead. Getting up off the wooden bar stool, I glanced around, looking for my stepfather. My heart thudded painfully against my ribs when I didn't find him sitting in the corner with his buddies.

I exited the clubhouse into the warm night air, exhaling the nerves fighting in the pit of my stomach like rabid dogs. The lights spilling through the windows broke the darkness and guided me over the rocky ground. The noise outside wasn't much better than inside because everyone was riding a high after the late-night run across the state line to bring back the stock that fell off the back of a truck into our willing hands.

Seeing no place else would be quieter, I swiped at the screen to accept my sister's call. "Hey, sis, not sure you can hear me with all the racket going on here," I shouted, hoping Calliope could hear me.

I was no farther than two steps deeper into the darkness when a piercing scream tried to rupture my ear drum. Heart lurching against my ribs, I squeezed the phone, blood turning to sludge in my veins as images filled my mind. "Calliope, where you at?" I shouted frantically over the pounding in my ears.

Moving toward my motorcycle, keys in my hand, it shook violently at the crashing sound and the next scream. "Home... stop him, Con!" The breathless, pain-filled words got the air backing up in my lungs at all the possibilities. Then the phone went dead.

Only one man would be in our trailer home, and red fiery rage chased the icy cold inside me. Things at home had gotten real tricky with Mom no longer alive and there to referee between Earl and us. Her third husband turned out to be a real scumbag, and as a member of Chosen Few, he thought he could lord it over Calliope and me.

He might have seniority in the club because of being part of the inner circle. Outside, that was a whole different ball game. One he was going to find out, and soon. I'd ignored him, played along with his dickish behavior to get the focus off Calliope. She was fourteen and Earl was her legal guardian because Mom had married the fucker. My hope had been he'd find a club whore and leave us the fuck alone before I'd have to step in. Being a patched member of Chosen Few meant I had to have all my brothers' backs. It made life damn fucking difficult. Now it appeared the line I'd been straddling was getting crossed.

Engine roaring to life, my brain on autopilot, I shoved the cell phone into my jeans pocket. There was no point in calling back. It would only waste time. Uncaring that I had neither helmet nor jacket on, I bounced on the seat of my motorcycle as I hit the ruts of the road that wasn't meant for speed.

I was breaking the speed limit by opening the throttle on the highway, but I didn't care. Nothing was going to stop me from getting to my sister. If the cops caught me, there'd be a chase because I wasn't pulling over, not even for the devil himself.

The seven miles from the clubhouse to my childhood home in a trailer park on the outskirts of town seemed to take forever. The lack of traffic in this part of town at night was normal. Folks didn't venture out after dark unless they were looking for trouble. The sight of the entrance to the trailer park kept my heart dancing in my chest. Head full of all the 'what ifs,' I'd barely pulled to a stop next to Earl's hog before I was off mine and charging inside.

It took two seconds to get my head to register the sights, sounds, and smells of pungent liquor and the coppery undertone of blood. Someone had trashed the place. Broken furniture lay haphazardly. The TV was facedown on the floor. The couple of wooden chairs we used were like fire sticks, but none of that caused the spit to dry in my mouth and my pulse to hit the stratosphere in record time.

In the middle of the trailer, blood covering her swollen and battered face, Earl pinned Calliope to the floor. Jean's down over his hairy ass, he grunted like a pig, muttering profanity as he raped my little sister. White furious rage came through me in a tidal wave. I bellowed and charged like a bull, murder on my mind.

Fueled by fury, I yanked him off my sister by the neck of his T-shirt as if he didn't weigh two hundred pounds. I swung him around before he could get his feet under him and punched him in his flushed and scratched face. He staggered, his legs trapped in his jeans, his cock flapping in the wind as he landed on his ass on the TV.

Driven by rage, I dove at him. Fury, like no other, chased away all logical thought as I landed hard enough to jar my own bones. My knee going for his groin, I slammed it down hard. The scream was deafening as I used all my weight to grind his cock and balls inside his body.

It barely registered that he wasn't hitting back as I launched my attack, pounding into his face with my fists. Blood spurted and hit my skin as bone crunched on bone, satisfying the ugly need to wipe him off the face of the planet. Unrelenting fury wouldn't stop with my sister right there, violated at this monster's hands. A part of me acknowledged she needed me, but the rage over his actions toward her wasn't letting go.

There was a noise outside, but none of it interfered with the black beast inside me. Arms heavy and hands throbbing with pain, sweat mixed with blood and blinded me to everything.

A predator scenting its prey's weakness, nothing else mattered while I punched into the now-unrecognizable face beneath me.

Jerking, my fist raised at the gentle touch to my shoulder, my head fired around, teeth bared at the fool stupid enough to interfere. One look at Calliope, and it felt like I'd plunged into icy water. Her appearance stole my breath.

She swayed, blood dripping down her legs as shaking hands held the torn dress over her breasts. She pleaded, "Con... stop... I can't lose you too."

The raggedness of her voice and bruised begging eyes made me suck in a breath, then another, pushing at the buzzing clouding my head. I registered the sounds of a commotion outside and sirens in the distance. "Fuck, which shithead called the cops?" I shouted out the still-open door, hearing voices hush and trailer doors slam.

I got to my feet, rubbing the backs of my hands on my T-shirt, ignoring the man on the floor like the trash he was.

Thoughts barreled into each other with the need to get out before the cops arrived. My gaze swept the destroyed trailer.

"You need to go. If the cops find you here, they'll arrest you." Her voice was stronger as she looked over to where Earl lay. "He's breathin', but that won't stop the law from wanting to take you in."

"I ain't leavin' here without you." Doing my best to shake off the anger that continued to pulse, I took Calliope's arm, figuring we had a minute or two by the sounds coming through the open door. "Grab your jacket and clothes to cover up, quick."

She didn't argue. Her legs wobbled as she walked to the back of the trailer where her room was. The regret that I couldn't comfort her right then, with the fear of losing her if the cops got here before we could get out, would come later. I'd already failed once at protecting her. Now I needed to figure out how to stop Earl from doing more damage.

I took a deep breath to hold back the sizzling anger before I glanced at Earl. The bile burned the back of my throat, but not from what I'd done. The bloodied face was mush, appearing as if I'd used a bat rather than my fists. He deserved no less. The bile was because I hadn't killed him.

I stepped around him, resisting kicking him in his swollen nuts. I crouched and rummaged through the jeans at his knees, searching for his wallet. It was payday. I flicked it open and smiled at the amount stuffed inside. I rose at the sound of Calliope coming, tucking the wallet into my back pocket.

Calliope, pale, bloody, and bruised, wearing a look of dignity, walked unsteadily toward me, holding out my spare helmet and jacket. She had her own on, along with jeans, a sloppy T-shirt, and her leather jacket.

The sirens getting louder stopped any conversation and the need to comfort her. Getting her out before the cops arrested me was the priority. No one was putting her in a state facility. That wasn't going to happen. "Let's go."

Outside, jacket and helmet on, I settled on my motorcycle. Curtains twitched, and I could sense the folks watching us. Calliope sat behind me and wrapped her arms around my waist. I didn't hesitate because I could see the flashing blue lights in the distance. Gravel spat, and I hit Earl's hog as I roared off toward the exit, taking a right in the opposite direction of the cop cars and my club members.

A favor owed by Dark Angels and the knowledge that their president's boyfriend was a lawyer made it an easy decision of where to head. Would Killer honor that I'd come down and protected Nutty, the club member who stayed behind with his daughter, River, when the other club members had gone to Washington a while back to deal with a problem?

In reality, the owed favor belonged to Chosen Few, not me directly. But right then, I couldn't see another option, and my brothers right now wouldn't be in a friendly mood, not with the law breathing down their necks. It wouldn't take long before the police figured out whose Earl was.

My hands tightened on the handlebars as the wind whipped through my open jacket. The worry nagged as the miles between Round Rock and Belton disappeared.

I groaned at what a shit show it was. *The lawyer has to see I have a case for beating up Earl, right? That him raping Calliope gave me the right to fuck him up?*

Thoughts and different scenes ran through my head with each passing mile. I didn't stop the urgency from getting someone to help Calliope, driving me on.

At some ungodly hour, I pulled up in front of Killer's tattoo shop and home. The neighborhood was quiet and suburban, not where anyone would expect a motorcycle club president to live. It screamed middle-class moms with families who did as they were told and had never known what it was like to be hungry a day in their lives. Even in the middle of the night, the place didn't give out the vibe that anything bad would happen there.

The lack of movement behind me drew my attention. "You doin' okay?"

"I think I need a hospital."

Barely louder than a whisper, I strained to hear her, terrified at what Earl might have done to her internally. "Can we go see Killer and his boyfriend first? I don't want them taking you from me." It was difficult not to let the fear show when she needed me to be strong.

The strangled moan sliced my gut as I got off the motorcycle, attempting not to jar her. Helmet off, I laid mine on my seat, then reached to take hers off, putting it next to mine. Carefully, I lifted her off the bike. With her feet on the ground, I slipped an arm around her waist and all but carried her up the path and steps to the house. I pressed the bell and didn't take my finger off, the sense of urgency riding me hard.

With each second, my heart ached at the possibility of them taking Calliope from me if Killer and his boyfriend refused to help. I wasn't one to pray. I didn't believe in such shit, but I prayed now as the seconds ticked down, and no one came to answer the door.

Where the fuck were they?

Chapter Two

Kyle

Rolling off the bed, I barely had the foresight to grab some underwear as I staggered to the door at Nutty's call and the constant sound of the doorbell, which I initially thought was in my dream. Squinting at my wristwatch in the bright hallway, I cursed. Who the fuck would knock at three a.m.? The brothers knew Linc was away. My stomach fluttered, and all sleepiness fled at what it could mean. Being in Dark Angels could bring trouble of its own.

"You expecting anyone?" I asked Nutty, who was looking as disheveled as me.

A door creaked open next to Nutty's, and River popped out of her room, her jammies all rumpled and her hair like a bird's nest. She rubbed at her eyes, yawning. "Who is it? They sound like they ain't goin' away, Ky. You don't think Poppy or Daddy have had an accident, does ya?"

Linc and Mason, her two dads, had left two days before to head to Las Vegas for a mini break that one of the other club members had gifted them.

I went over and tapped the end of her nose. "No, I don't. The cops would have called us if there was a problem." I hoped I was right. "I'll go check it out."

Nutty's brows rose as she tugged River to her, concern in her eyes. Her gaze dropped to my body. "Dressed like that?"

I glanced down at the boxer briefs concealing little. Fuck!

I headed back into Linc's bedroom, where I was staying while he was away. I'd offered when he'd mentioned three times in a conversation about having never left River for five days. His usual was three days max. It was an easy offer when I could roll out of bed and head straight to work with no effort.

Joggers on, I didn't stop to find a T-shirt because the persistent fucker never let up on the bell for a second. My stomach churned much like a washing machine at the insistent press of the bell. Whoever was on the other side of the door wasn't letting up. They either had a death wish coming to Linc's door like this or were desperate. Neither was a good option at three a.m.

Nutty and River had remained in the hallway, both looking fully alert. "You both stay up here. Any trouble, lock yourselves in one room and call Sid."

At Nutty's nod, I headed downstairs, turning the lights on as I went. The shape of figures through the glass didn't give me any clues about who was on the other side of the door. I could handle myself one-on-one if need be, but two-on-one was definitely a big ask. Standing to my full height, I took a deep breath and unlocked the door. The air left my lungs so fast that my head got dizzy as I stared at the large man in front of me... holding a teenage girl. One who was as white as a ghost if I discarded the blood and bruises covering her face and neck.

Pulse hammering in my throat, my head ran faster than my hog at full throttle. Had he done that to her?

"I need help," the man I recognized from Shorty's all those months ago ground out. The raspy voice sounded as if he'd swallowed glass.

Dark eyes met mine, and there was anger and fear.

"You do that?" The sinister edge to my voice could more than match Linc's when pissed at someone.

The fire came fast into his dark eyes. They blazed at me, and regardless of the attraction I felt toward the large guy buzzing under my skin, I'd never show interest in an asshole who'd beat up women.

"Her stepfather. I found him raping her. She's my little sister, Calliope. Killer owes Dog a favor, and I'm here to collect it."

The fear he didn't keep control of in the quiver in his voice had me stepping back to let them in. My gaze narrowed, lingering on his bloodied knuckles and the leather jacket. Pulse back to thudding painfully, I nodded at the teenage girl, who could barely stand with her legs shaking.

The door hadn't closed properly when there was a noise behind me.

"What's going on?" Nutty asked, her bare feet slapping on the wood behind me.

I looked sideways when Nutty came forward, still wearing the massive T-shirt she slept in, her legs bare. Her spiky, dark hair was a little more tamed on one side where she'd lain on it. "What did I say?" I questioned in exasperation.

Nutty gave me what appeared to be an unrepentant grin before it disappeared when she took in the couple in front of us. "I know you. Conall, isn't it? You came and stayed here when everyone went up to Washington."

My mouth hung open for a moment, then snapped shut. He'd been here in Belton, stayed in Linc's house? How did I not know this?

"You know him?" I'd mooned over the guy for months, and Nutty and Linc knew him! What the ever-loving fuck.

The girl clung to the guy, her head lolling to the side, distracting me.

Nutty didn't answer me. Instead, she stroked a gentle hand over the girl's silvery blonde hair. "Come in. Come in. Do you need us to call a doctor?"

The girl's pain-filled moans with each movement sent shivers down my spine. The man, Conall, held her closer to him, a deep scowl appearing. "I don't wanna take her to the hospital. They'll ask too many questions and wanna take her from me."

A look passed between Nutty and me. There was a lot the guy wasn't saying, and I could add up as much as Nutty. She had friends who worked at the hospital. Would they come here and help? Neither of us wanted the sheriff's deputies here when Linc was away.

"I have a friend who's a nurse. She might help." As Nutty spoke, I looked at the man, who looked distrustful, judging by the deep furrows grooved into the side of his mouth. It took his sister moaning once more to get him to nod.

"I'll help you get her upstairs." I closed the door and locked it, then turned to help. But Conall wore an expression that suggested he'd break my hand if I so much as laid a finger on his sister.

"I've got her," he growled and, with care, guided the girl to the stairs, following Nutty.

The back of his leather jacket had a patch, revealing the truth of his affiliation.

At the top, River stood watching us. I sighed and hoped Linc wouldn't kick my ass too hard for letting these two—who had trouble written all over them—into the house. I'd been labeled a bleeding heart more than once. "River, go on back to bed. I'll be in to tuck you back in."

Her little chin popped out. "Why? I know Conall, and he's nice. I like him. He played with me when he came to look after me when Poppy and Daddy went to Washington." River glanced at the girl Conall held up, a frown marring her small forehead. "Someone did something bad to her. I wanna help too. Poppy says you should always help those who needs it. Conall helped Poppy, so I'm gonna help Conall and his girlfriend."

"Sister," I corrected, not sure why I felt the need to point out it wasn't his girlfriend to a six-year-old. Seeing that I wasn't going to persuade her differently about helping with the light in her eyes matching the one her Poppy wore often, I gave an exasperated sigh and pointed to the bathroom door. "Get the first aid box Linc has in the bathroom. I think I saw it buried under some towels."

"Okay, Kyle." She skipped off, but not before I witnessed her satisfied grin.

In the living room, Nutty placed cushions under the girl's blonde head after her brother helped settle her on the couch. I didn't miss her wince or the groan of pain.

What damage had the fucker done to her before her brother stopped him? Judging by the swollen knuckles Conall sported, I was betting the guy had his face rearranged. But had he gone further?

I wasn't sure what I'd do if I found someone raping a family member.

"I'll go call Liz. Give me a couple of minutes."

The second Nutty was out the door, I gave Conall a pointed stare, listening for River coming. "Talk now. I wanna know what mess you're bringin' to Linc's door before Nutty or River comes back."

The guy took his sweet time, crouching in front of his sister, not looking at me. "I punched him about until his face resembled a pizza." It was a flat delivery, emotionless, and goosebumps sprung up over my chest and arms.

"You know if anyone called the cops?"

That got him looking back at me. "Yeah, the trailer park we live...lived in, the neighbors called the cops. The sirens were blaring, and I took off before they got there."

I breathed a little easier, knowing he hadn't actively evaded the cops. "Where's your motorcycle parked?" My head was already working out what we needed to do to stop folks from asking questions.

"On the road outside."

River appeared, carrying the large box Linc kept for medical emergencies. The box was a struggle for her to carry as it filled her little arms. "Kyle, I got it."

She staggered a little, so I went to her. I ran a hand over her head, smiling. "Thanks' kiddo."

Before I opened it, Nutty appeared, and the look of relief got rid of some of the tension running over my shoulders. "Liz is on her way. Should be here in ten minutes." Nutty kneeled at Conall's side, reaching for Calliope's hand. "Shit, she's freezing. Kyle, go grab a spare blanket from my closest."

Doing as she asked, I was back holding the blanket a minute later. Nutty took it. "Go make some hot tea. Put plenty of sugar in it. I think she's going into shock."

Off again, I used the task of making tea to stop stressing about what could happen if Liz said Calliope needed medical attention.

Carrying a tray, I shouldered the door open and went to the table next to the couch. Nutty was talking in a soothing voice as she used one of the wet wipes that must have been in the medical box to clean Calliope's face. "Should you be doing that?" I asked without thinking.

River, who watched with open curiosity on the seat across from the couch, twisted to look at me. "Why? She's only helping to make Calliope feel better."

How the hell was I supposed to answer that? "Sometimes you need evidence to help stop the bad people."

"Oh, you mean like when I went and spoke to the judge person about Poppy and what I'd seen when Nola said he was bad when he wasn't?"

"Yes, like that," I answered, relieved but on the inside squirming when Nutty aimed a hard stare in my direction at the quiver in River's voice. "Listen, I think it's best if I move your motorcycle and put it in the garage."

Conall didn't look at me as a hand went into his jacket pocket and he tossed the key in my direction. I caught it and hated myself for the tingling that came from holding the key that had been snug and warm against his body.

Key in hand, I went to the bedroom to find a T-shirt and put on my sneakers. Minutes later, outside in the darkness, I shut the garage door hurriedly at the sound of a car approaching. A thin layer of sweat coated my skin when I swung around, hoping my face revealed none of my thoughts as I aimed a friendly smile at the driver parking their car in the space that I'd just moved the motorcycle from. The redheaded girl I glimpsed in the streetlight was one I'd seen a time or two with Nutty, and it settled my pounding heart.

Plastering a smile on my face, I waited for Liz, who was always friendly, to get out of the compact car. She was petite and curvy, dressed in leggings and a baggy sweater. Her hair was in a high pony which bounced as she moved to retrieve a large bag from the back seat. My gaze went to the bag, and my heart jerked hard, bringing back—not that it had gone far—the reality of what and who was in Linc's home and place of business.

"Hey, Kyle, been a while."

"It has, and I'm sorry we're meeting under these circumstances," I whispered, looking about as we walked back to the house.

"Nutty didn't say much. I got the feeling it's a fucked-up situation."

The matter-of-fact way she spoke helped, her voice no higher than mine. "It is."

Chapter Three

Conall

I let out another breath of relief when Kyle, who'd returned—thankfully wearing more clothes—with the nurse, Liz, left with River to tuck her back into bed. The child had a will of steel, and it took both Liz and Nutty explaining that Calliope needed privacy to get her to leave with Kyle.

My head was mush, and I was still recovering from the shock I'd received seeing Kyle standing in Killer's home, bare-chested, and giving me a fierce stare that could rival both Killer and Dog. How had I missed that Kyle was a member of Dark Angels? He had to be. There was no way Killer would leave his daughter with someone he didn't trust implicitly. When I'd stayed to watch over River, Killer had pointed out exactly what he was entrusting me with and what he'd do to me if anything happened to River.

How long had Kyle been a member of Dark Angels? Was he about when I'd come to Belton?

It was far easier to keep my gaze on Calliope and shut out questions that had no business filling my head while my sister was hurt.

What color she'd maintained had bleached to milk-white, making the livid bruising a harsh reminder she'd fought to stop the fucker from touching her.

"Calliope, I need to take your clothes off to see what I'm dealing with." Liz glanced at Nutty. "It would be better to do that on a bed."

"You can use mine," Nutty replied without hesitation.

"Conall, can you carry your sister for me? I don't want her walking."

"Con," Calliope gasped, her eyelids fluttering madly.

"It's all right, sis. I gotcha." Every moan and groan dug deeper into my soul as I scooped her up and followed Nutty out of the room, the nurse close behind, her bag banging off my leg a time or two.

Nutty yanked up the covers and smoothed them over, bringing to attention the rude awakening I'd given them all. "You can put her down now."

A hand touched my jacket, and I glanced at the redheaded nurse. "What?" I gritted out.

"I need some privacy, as does your sister. I promise I'll take good care of her."

I met Liz's stare, one that never wavered as I gave her a warning. "Calli, you happy for me to go? I won't go far, I swear."

When I met Calliope's gaze, she nodded slowly. It took all her effort as her eyes drifted shut a moment later.

"Don't hurt her."

"I'll do my best, but I won't promise because what I need to do when examining her may cause added discomfort, briefly at least." She held up a hand as I parted my lips to interrupt her. "I can't give her anything for the pain until I know the extent of her injuries. They could mask a more serious problem." The lack of false promises helped make the vomit coating the back of my throat stay put for now.

I stood in the hallway at a loss as blood burned through my veins with the fury of feeling so helpless. My aching fists clenched and unclenched repeatedly.

There was a noise, and Kyle appeared out of a doorway I knew was River's bedroom. He paused at the sight of me, looking at the shut door of Nutty's bedroom. "They moved into Nutty's room?"

"Yeah," I gritted out, struggling to be civil.

"Wanna drink?" Kyle asked in a low voice as he moved from River's door toward me. "I'm thinkin' you could do with a stiff one."

"Where's Killer?" I asked instead of answering him. If I drank liquor now, I wasn't sure I'd want to stop drowning my sorrows. Until Liz figured out what Calliope needed, I couldn't afford the luxury.

"He's away with Mason. They're on a five-day trip to Las Vegas. They won't be back till Friday."

"Fuck!" I snapped angrily. I might not have three days to get my shit figured out.

Kyle, who'd taken a step, pulled up short. "You think the cops will look for you? Won't your brothers have your back?"

I eyed the man I didn't know and weighed how much I could trust him. Lust couldn't play any part in Calliope's situation or mine. "They will, as long as it doesn't draw an unwanted shit storm raining down on them. They got...stuff going on that don't need scrutiny at the club." The fat wallet in my back pocket reminded me exactly how pissed Dog would be if my actions rocked the side businesses that brought in cash for the club and its members. Dog gave no one a free pass for fucking that up, and I'd seen what that meant for one member. The removal of their patch was the least of it.

"Then you'll need a place to stay until the heat dies down." It wasn't a question, so it didn't warrant an answer. Kyle ran a hand through his untidy hair, and the tattoo sleeve—a thing of beauty with many distinct elements—showed off the enormous eye on his inner bicep. The 3-D effect and design made it appear lifelike and gave the illusion it would start blinking any second. "My apartment is free and has a couple of spare rooms. It's nothing special, but it's got cable and everything you'll need."

I aimed a confused look at him. "What?" Had he just offered his home?

A coat of color infused his cheeks. The hand went back to running through the thick, dark hair. "My place. You can crash there till Linc and Mason get back."

A fluttering started in the bottom of my stomach, along with a weird warmth in the center of my chest. Disconcerted, I frowned. "Why would you offer me your place? You don't know me."

He shrugged and walked past me down the hallway. I grabbed his arm and stopped him. He looked at the hand, then back at me. "Why?" I demanded, needing an answer.

"'Cause you need it." He nodded toward Nutty's closed door. "And she needs it. What more reason is there than that? Brothers help each other out. You helped Linc when he needed it. He's my brother, so..." He shook off my hand and disappeared down the hallway into the kitchen.

I was rooted to the spot, unable to figure out what his angle was. No one did nothing for no one in my world unless they wanted a favor in return. What would Kyle want from me? And would it be too high a price to pay if I took him up on his offer?

I wasn't sure how long I stood staring at the empty hallway, contemplating Kyle's angle, before Nutty's door opened and Liz appeared. "Conall, you can come back in now."

Stealing a breath, I stepped into the room behind her. I shuddered at how fragile Calliope looked tucked in the bed, appearing as if she was asleep. "I've given her a sedative. Do you want me to lay it all out for you?"

"Yup." My gaze went to Liz, and I straightened my shoulders.

"She has extensive bruising to the insides of her thighs, over her chest, and stomach besides what you can see on her neck and face. I've taken pictures of all the marks on her, with her consent," she added quickly when I bristled, glowering at her. "I know she's a minor, but I didn't want to stop and add to her trauma. She has vaginal tears, but there didn't appear to be any semen. I have swabbed for all the standard sexually transmitted diseases and DNA if you want to press charges against whoever raped her. I've drawn blood for testing too. I have a friend who works in the lab who'll process this for me without asking too many questions. Right now, she needs to rest and recover. Then she's gonna need someone to speak to who deals with this kind of assault and trauma." She spoke matter-of-factly, though there was sympathy in her eyes.

"She don't need the hospital then?" I needed that laid out, as it was my biggest fear.

"No, but if you want to go after the fucker that did this to her and give credit to the rape kit I've taken, the hospital is the best place for her."

"The information you get from your guy, will you be able to give that to me?" Dog would want it if he was going to have my and Calliope's backs. The hospital staff would only want to take my sister from me, and that wasn't happening. Dog would deal with Earl with some club justice. That was the only kind that mattered to me.

"I can." She glanced at Nutty, and silent communication passed between them.

Nutty nodded. "I can come and get it from you and give it to Kyle if that works best?"

Liz was nodding before Nutty finished talking. "That works." Liz touched the sleeve of the jacket I still wore. "It's best we aren't seen together. If anyone at the hospital figures out I did this, my job could be at risk." A laugh that wasn't very humorous was followed by a grimace. "Patched members of any club here aren't seen in a positive light," she explained.

Understanding the risk she'd taken for Calliope and me, left me floundering with what to say. Thanks didn't seem enough. "Nutty has my number, and I've left some pain meds for Calliope. I'll be back tomorrow evening after my shift to check in and see how she's doin'."

"Thanks," I muttered, heat blooming in my cheeks when she gave me a flirty smile.

"You're both welcome. Sorry I can't stay any longer. I need to get going because I'm due to go to work shortly."

Nutty helped her pack her stuff away, and they both left me alone with Calliope. I sat on the edge of the bed and stroked a hand over her silky hair. She murmured, "Con," and snuggled into my hand.

"I'm here, Calli. I gotcha. We're gonna be fine," I said, infusing all my determination. One that had gotten me through a shitty life. What was one more shit storm to weather alone?

I groaned as I moved, my back protesting my slumped position. It took a second to realize I'd fallen asleep sitting up next to Calliope. One glance at the pretty female room revealed Nutty—if she had returned—hadn't stayed. The closed curtains didn't shut out the fact it was full daylight outside. I ran both hands over my face, rubbing away the tiredness and grit from my eyes. My tongue ran over my teeth, and I groaned with the need for something to drink.

I eased myself off the bed, trying not to disturb Calliope, whose chest was moving rhythmically, suggesting she was deeply asleep. I stretched to get rid of the kinks, swallowing the groan from the move when my back popped repeatedly.

Glancing at the door, I tilted my head, listening for any sounds. Hearing nothing, I walked out into the hallway, checking my watch. I blinked, stopping mid-stride. Twelve o'clock? How can it be so late?

Where was everyone?

In the hallway, there were voices below me and a phone ringing, then stopping. I walked to the stairs and peered down. Seeing nothing, I debated what I should do. Coffee, a shower, and feeding Calliope were on the list, but this wasn't my place, and it didn't feel right just helping myself to stuff.

I stood so long that my back complained about my position. Looking down and over the railing, about to move back, I caught movement below on the next floor.

"Remember to follow the care instructions this time, Jonas. I ain't listenin' to your ole lady harp on about how she couldn't get any. My ears are still burnin' from the row she gave me last time. Gettin' tats on your hips is all good as long as you look after them properly."

There was a chuckle, and a guy with streaked dirty-blond hair appeared wearing a sheepish expression. "I was working extra to pay for the tattoo so she'd stop bitchin' about the cost, and I was plum tuckered when I got home and forgot."

Kyle's laugher was deep and full-bodied. "Then get your ole lady to do the taking care part. That way, she won't rag on my ass."

Jonas slapped Kyle on the shoulder, drawing my attention to the broadness and fit of the preppy button-down he was wearing. Jonas nodded before thumping down the stairs and disappearing. Kyle worked for Killer. How had I missed that on my visits to the shop to get Killer's ink on me?

As if Kyle felt my stare, he glanced up, and his gaze locked with mine. His expression wasn't easy to read as a furrow appeared between his brows and the smile he'd worn disappeared. "You're awake. There's coffee in the pot on the stove. There's the makings for sandwiches in the refrigerator. I'll be up once I've cleaned up to talk." On that, he disappeared from view, and I was the one frowning at the abruptness in the way Kyle had spoken.

It seemed I'd pissed him off. But the dark circles under his eyes were all my fault, so who could blame him for being pissed? It didn't sit well with me, but I could see little that would change it. The attraction I'd felt the first time I'd seen him at Shorty's waited like a cat watching a mouse, ready to catch me out. Something that wouldn't do me any favors after seeing what kind of guy he was interested in. I wasn't preppy, and I wasn't willing to change, even if the guy was hot as fuck.

Trudging into the kitchen with the coffee calling my name, I considered if Kyle was about to take back the offer of his place. I hadn't answered him. Would he take that as a no?

A knot formed in my stomach as I went to the coffeepot.

Chapter Four

Kyle

I'd felt the weight of Conall's stare while talking to Jonas. It had taken everything in me to act normal. When I'd glanced up and met Conall's beautiful gray-green eyes, it set off the nerves that hadn't been far away since I'd answered the door to him. With him just above my head the entire morning, I'd stressed about what he was doing when I was clueless about what, if anything, he'd do after he'd disappeared into Nutty's room and hadn't ventured out to talk about what came next. Not that I'd been spying. I hadn't. There'd been little point in returning to bed once Liz had left at five o'clock and my first client was at eight, so I'd showered and hovered in case they'd needed anything. Anything at all. That was the only reason I'd ventured into the hallway about a gazillion times to check.

Nutty had bunked with River to catch another couple of hours, then she'd taken River to Mina's as planned. River had been good and promised to say nothing about our early-morning callers. River was a switched-on kid for a six-year-old. Linc had taught her not to discuss personal stuff with strangers, not that Mina was a stranger, but she wasn't family. Nutty had told me not to stress, but it was hard not to. She wasn't aware I'd offered Conall my apartment. I'd held that bit back. It wasn't like he'd said yes, even if he didn't have many options. I was working on figuring out if he had trust issues or if life had given him hard options, so he expected that all the time.

There was something about him...

I sighed again at my lameness. "Admit it, the man was hard to get out of your head the first time. Now he's damn near wedged his ass in there and is refusing to budge!" I muttered to myself, then glanced at the door to make sure no one had come up to use the kitchen on this floor. Work should have helped keep my mind occupied and away from Conall. I had a full list of clients for the day who needed me to be focused. Why was it so damn hard to do that with Conall hanging around upstairs?

Jeez, you're a dumbass.

The problem was, what do I do now? He was upstairs, looking all sexy and rumpled. Should I honor the offer I rashly gave the night before or the early hours of this morning? I wanted to, but who was I kidding? In the light of day, the offer I'd given without thought now seemed purely selfish with my interest in getting to know Conall... in every sense.

Yes, his sister had been my first thought of benefiting from having a place to stay. But I couldn't ignore that Conall would be in my home, using my things, and for a bizarre reason I didn't want to think too hard about, that gave me more than a spark of pleasure. Did that make me a bad person when his sister should be my first concern?

I groaned over the answer that sprang instantly to mind. I was going to hell. There were no two ways about it.

Cleaning up the counter and putting away the inks I had used, I gave myself a few minutes to gather my thoughts. The only problem was that I wasn't sure how it would make any difference when I'd already gone over the situation more than once. Realistically, they couldn't stay at Linc's place. Too many people came and went, with the tattoo shop being part of the house. That really only left my place.

You keep believing that.

With nothing left to clean, I heaved a sigh and, with slumped shoulders, headed out the door and up the stairs. I walked into the kitchen and paused at the sight of Conall sitting at Linc's kitchen table. The leather jacket he'd worn was slung over the back of the seat. He was wearing a black shirt over his broad back. The expanse of it made my palms tingle with the desire to run a hand over it to see if it was as muscular as it appeared. It reminded me of the first night we'd met—if it could be called a meeting, the only conversation had been one word I had spoken.

My gaze swept the table, and a furrow appeared between my brows. The only thing that sat in front of Conall was a coffee mug. "You're not hungry?"

He didn't look in my direction as he picked up the cup and sipped the steaming black liquid.

Okay, not the talkative type then.

I walked to the kitchen counter and grabbed a cup, filling it with coffee. I added some sweetener and went and took a seat next to Conall. "At some point, you're gonna have to talk. Or is it that you are a man of few words who prefers to communicate another way?" I joked, hoping to ease a little of the tension I could feel between us.

His head moved slowly in my direction. His choppily cut hair shifted around his striking face. The stubble on his jaw added to the bad-boy appearance when his more gray than green eyes met mine. There was a storm brewing inside him, waiting to be unleashed. I was perverse enough to want it.

I picked up the cup and sipped the hot, bitter liquid for something to do. I had left the coffee on the stove too long, but I wasn't in the mood to make any more, so I took another sip.

The silent man beside me held all my attention as his gaze never wavered. It felt like a game of cat and mouse, only I wasn't sure who was playing which part.

I remained quiet, holding my cup, and waited him out. The minutes ticked by as he focused back on his coffee and sipped. I wasn't sure how much time had passed before he glanced sideways again. The memory of our first meeting was there, and how his eyes had tugged at me with past sorrows. He hadn't lived an easy life. I'd have bet my hands on it.

I held my breath and waited to see what he would say.

"Did you mean what you said last night about letting us stay at your place for a few days?"

"I did. Being here with so many people around ain't an option. Then when Linc gets back Friday, he'll maybe have some ideas about what comes next for you and your sister. Have you reached out to Dog to explain what happened? Find out if the cops are sniffing around, looking for you?"

A deep furrow appeared between his brows. "Not yet."

"Why not? Surely he'll be understanding?"

"The person who did this to my sister was a member of Chosen Few. He's part of the inner circle and one of Dog's good friends. So it's complicated." Each word sounded like they were being dragged from him.

"What the fuck!" I got off the seat, unable to sit still at the very idea that a brother wouldn't have Conall's back over this.

I jabbed a finger in the air. "If this was Linc, he would go after whoever it was and show them it ain't acceptable to rape a defenseless girl. Whoever the fucker was that did this to your sister, they need to get club justice. No one should be exempt from that. They should make them pay."

"Life ain't always that simple. There isn't just black and white. In our world, there are forty fucking thousand colors of gray to wade through. You're a club member. You should know this!" he growled, sounding pissed off. His eyes fired the same warning shots he'd aimed at me last night.

I was never good at stepping back. "I know that," I snapped back. "Club justice is that, justice. There is no way your brothers wouldn't have your back for this. And if they don't, they ain't your brother's!"

"You know jack shit." The chair smashed backward as he stomped toward me, his nose nearly touching mine as he glowered. I could smell the coffee on his breath. "What I know is that I beat the fuck out of a club member, and for that, I'll bring the law down on them because I didn't do it at the clubhouse. I left my dirty laundry out for everyone to see, and that is unacceptable. So whatever Dog will do to me, he'll believe I deserve it."

Conall's chest heaved, his breath hitting my face in short bursts. Nothing in his voice showed that he didn't believe what he was saying. The absolute finality in his tone and the look in his eyes turned my blood cold. Was Dog that much of a hard-faced bastard he'd come down hard on Conall?

I'd met Dog once, and the man came across as decent, unlike the person Conall was painting a picture of right now. Was I wrong about Dog? I couldn't see it. But then he'd been more than happy to help Linc with his problem of clearing house. There was no more time for conversation when a soft, lyrical voice called out from the hallway, "Con, where you at?"

A softness came over his hard expression and then was gone as he aimed his gaze at me. "You ain't to mention any of this conversation in front of my sister. I don't need her worryin'."

He got an inch closer, his nose now touching mine. "Understood?" His voice was low and sinister, his gaze unwavering.

The urge to kiss him was far too tempting, so I forcibly stepped back from the challenge in his eyes, knowing now was not the time or place. "Go check on your sister. We'll finish this later." When there wouldn't be any interruptions, I promised myself. I hadn't missed the flare of desire in his eyes. I also hadn't missed how he closed himself off straight after.

Damn.

Conall called out, "Comin' sis," and then he walked out of the kitchen without a backward look. It was something I was coming to dislike. Going back to the table, I picked up my cup and dumped the contents down the sink, rinsing it out and placing it on the drying rack.

There was a murmured conversation coming through the open door. I debated with myself for a second whether I should go out into the hallway, and then Nutty decided for me when she appeared in the doorway. "Your next client is here, and he's looking nervous as fuck. I think a ghost would have more color than this guy. I've taken him to your room and left him with a sweet drink to see if it helps." She slapped my arm and laughed. "Good luck with him." Her laughter followed her out of the room.

"Great," I mumbled under my breath. This was all I needed, a fainter.

I kept out of Conall's way for the rest of the day and stayed in my room until the last client left. Exhausted but pleased that

I hadn't fucked up any of the tattoos, I rubbed at the back of my neck, where the muscles ached from having to look down and concentrate harder than normal. I took pride in my work, and it wasn't often anything could mess with my head, but it would appear Conall was one of those oddities.

It wasn't like I didn't know he could mess with my head because I'd spent the last few months letting him do just that from one brief encounter.

Give the fuck up. It's not like he's interested!

Then why did he look interested earlier?

He was angry!

The conversation in my head continued, and I pretended like it wasn't me just going around in circles.

Downstairs, after cleaning and putting everything away, I nodded at Nutty and leaned on the reception desk. As usual, she tucked the phone between her shoulder and ear as she chatted away. The reception area was empty, not that I expected anyone to be hanging around now. It was after six. Troy and Ali, the two other tattoo artists, had left an hour ago.

I hadn't missed how they'd thrown me odd looks when they'd popped in to see me between clients. That they'd noticed I wasn't myself meant I'd have to try harder tomorrow. I hoped that with Conall at my place, if he was still interested, the temptation to head up and see him, even if it was to get one of his angry snarls or glares, would cease.

When Nutty and I had come down for work this morning, we'd had a quick conversation before my first client about if we should tell anyone about Conall's arrival with his sister. The issue was neither of us wanted to bring trouble from another club down on us. Linc had a good relationship with Chosen Fews' president Dog, and messing with that wasn't an option. So until Linc returned, we were going to keep quiet and hope nothing happened between then and Friday.

Off the phone, she grinned at me. "You look as tired as I feel."

I self-consciously ran a hand through my hair, then tugged at my button-down, straightening, far too aware of what was happening next. "I'm not too bad. Did you get any chance to check on Calliope throughout the day?"

She nodded. "She's doing okay. Doesn't look so pale, though she looks like a truck hit her. I ordered some food for them, and when I checked later, they'd both eaten. What are we gonna do with them? We ain't got enough bedrooms for them to stay here."

I kept my smile in place with difficulty. "I offered them my apartment."

Her eyes widened, then narrowed. "You did? When did that happen? Far as I know, you ain't left your room except at lunchtime."

"Last night," I muttered, trying not to shrink under her stink eye.

"You never said this morning," she accused, her cheeks flushing.

"He never said yes," I answered, way too defensively.

One brow arched. "Is that right?"

"It is. So, let's go figure out how to get them to my place without being seen." I stomped off, praying she'd let the subject drop.

She called out after me, "Don't think this topic of conversation is over."

I hunched and muttered to myself, "Yeah, yeah." She was just like my Mom. She had to know everything!

Chapter Five

Conall

The cell phone on the kitchen counter rang, and I jerked in my seat at the familiar ringtone echoing through the small area Kyle had just off the kitchen. My insides twisted into painful knots as I stared at it for long seconds, unmoving.

There'd been no word for the last two days since I'd texted Dog to test how deep the shit was. Nothing, just dead air. The ringtone suggested it was one member of Chosen Few, but which one.

"That cell phone ain't gonna answer itself," called Calliope from the living room couch where she'd been channel suffering and eating popcorn most of the afternoon.

She muted the sound when I glanced over to where she was sitting, and my eyebrows rose at her snippy tone. Nutty had found some clothes that fit, sort of. Calliope was tall for her age, at five-eight, and Nutty had to be three inches shorter. The sweatshirt was fine, but the leggings that sat halfway up her calves were a little odd-looking. "I think I preferred you when you were quiet," I stated with no heat, undecided about answering the cell phone.

I wasn't a coward. It pissed me off no one had bothered to reach out sooner. Kyle had suggested contacting Rattlesnake, an original member of Dark Angels who moved to be with a girlfriend close to Austin. Killer had put in a good word with Dog, and he'd joined Chosen Few.

I'd vetoed that idea, not wanting to alert the club when the hours had turned into days and I had too much to lose. It felt like the right call, but now I wasn't so sure.

Calliope groaned as she got off the couch when the ringing persisted. I resisted getting up to help her because she'd attempted to bite my head off earlier when I'd suggested I help her to the bathroom. Although she looked less swollen in the face, the bruising was more evident in an array of blacks, blues, and purples. The bruising on her legs and lower body made it hard for her to get about without pain, something Liz said would take a few days to change due to the damage he'd inflicted.

When I met her gaze, her expression was full of concern. Her eyes traveled to the ringing object I had yet to move toward. "They'll get pissed at you if you don't answer."

"Ya think? But they've taken their sweet time to get in touch. That does not bode well for me either." It was the conclusion I'd come to the day before. I hadn't put too much in the message. It was brief and to the point: Earl raped Calliope. What more was there to say?

I hadn't indicated where I was hiding. Or that I'd come to Killer to claim the favor with the man not due back until the next day. I wasn't going to count my damn chickens until I'd spoken to him to see if he'd help me.

The ringing stopped, only to start again. Calliope reached the counter and tapped the screen. "Hello?"

"That you, Calliope?" asked Rattlesnake on speakerphone. Fuck!

Did they know I'd come to Belton? Rattlesnake was one of the newer recruits and someone I had a lot of time for. He didn't talk bullshit like some of the other brothers, and he'd gained Dog's trust quickly for it. I hadn't expected him to be the person to reach out.

I glared at her, and she shrugged. "Yup."

"Where you at, brother?"

The hesitation lasted a second as I debated whether it was best to keep quiet. "I'm right here." I decided facing what was coming was how I'd dealt with life. I didn't see any point in changing now with so much at stake.

"Where's here?"

"That ain't important right now. Whassup?"

A sharp laugh came through the speaker. "You're askin' me that?"

"Yup. I messaged Dog two days ago, and then I'm getting nothing but dead air. So whassup?"

There was the sound of scraping, then the noise of a door opening and closing. "You brought a ton of crap down on the club. The cops have been hangin' around like flies on shit, poking their noses into everythin'." I shivered at what his lowered voice meant.

"Does Dog know you're calling me?"

The pause was noticeable and answered my suspicions before he said, "No."

Breath hissed past my teeth. Was I being cut out before I explained myself? Before I proved what a scumbag Earl was? "Earl raped my sister!" I snapped angrily, then regretted it when Calliope winced. "He got what he deserved. The fucker should be dead." The utter seriousness in my tone caused Calliope's face to drain of color. A sheen of tears appeared in her colorful eyes as she held out the phone.

When I took it, she walked stiffly toward the bedroom, a door closing quietly behind her as I silently cursed for losing my cool in front of her. She was the one he'd laid hands on and had to deal with how that made her feel. I promised myself I'd apologize after the call.

"He nearly was. You smashed his face in good. His airway wasn't so great. They had to stick a tube in to help him breathe. He hasn't woken up yet to tell the cops anythin', something about brain swelling. They still ain't a hundred percent sure he's gonna make it. The cops are looking for the next of kin to inform. Dog told them you and your sister were away visiting family. They weren't satisfied, I could tell. They'll be looking for your cell number, which Dog didn't give them, so be warned."

There was the sound of stubble being scratched before he continued, "If he dies, they'll be lookin' at you for murder. The interfering fuckers in the trailer park are keeping their mouths shut for now. Let's hope it stays that way."

Too wound up to keep sitting, I stood and strode around the living area, hoping the peaceful vibe would work on my anxiety. Kyle's description of the place being nothing special was far from what I was used to. This place was sheer luxury to me. A large sectional couch took up one wall and was big enough for me to lie down fully on it. Thick cushions made it too easy to dose off. The walls were a muted green, and the artwork on them was all tattoo designs, some of which graced the upper part of Kyle's body.

The rest of the furniture was a pale wood that was the same as the kitchen. The place had a homely vibe. It was the only word I'd decided fit the place.

"You still with me?"

Rattlesnake's question brought my attention away from the room and back to the call. "I'm here. I don't know what you want me to say. He raped Calli. I got evidence. Pictures and shit, and I'll have test results from the rape kit the nurse took to prove it. When I found him on top of her, what else was I supposed to do, let him fucking finish and roll off? What would you have done if you'd found a scumbag raping your girl?" I demanded.

"I ain't on Earl's side, you dick, but things here are bad. There's talk you walked away with Earl's take," he growled, harsh breathing coming through the speaker. "I'm risking a damn ass-kicking for reachin' out and talkin' to you about just how deep the shit is you got yourself into. I was callin' to suggest maybe a trip to Belton would be a good idea. Mason's solid and knows his way around the law. He helped Killer. I bet he'd help you too." His voice had dropped further as if he was worried someone would hear him.

The worry resurfaced faster than a wave hitting the shore that Rattlesnake had figured out I was in Belton. My pulse leaped, and the hand holding the phone trembled before I got control. I wasn't worried about the money. Earl owed it to Calliope. "You think they'd help me?"

"I do. If you aren't happy about goin' there, then call the shop." There was a pause and some rustling. "Listen, I gotta go, but I'll keep you updated on anythin' I hear. Keep safe, brother."

The call ended, and I stared out the apartment window into the darkness.

In the daylight, the view wasn't of anything other than buildings, and initially, I'd felt trapped inside. We'd arrived in the dead of night so as not to draw suspicion. The first night, the scent of Kyle teasing my nose prevented me from getting much shut-eye. I didn't have any distractions other than my thoughts, and the fresh smell of Kyle was way more appealing. Then there were the tattoo pictures hanging around, giving me ideas I shouldn't be having when he clearly wasn't into leather-clad bad boys. I'd watched him trying to get the guy at

Shorty's to notice him. The idiot hadn't shown any genuine interest, and the way he'd looked down his nose at Kyle made my fists clench with the desire to punch his sneering mouth.

I'd done none of that. Instead, I'd stepped into Kyle's path when I saw him heading in my direction because I seemed to enjoy teasing myself with what wasn't for me. But for a moment, I'd thought I saw interest, then considered I'd been mistaken when I glanced at the preppy boy at the bar.

Unsure how long I'd been standing there recalling what Kyle had worn that first night and what I'd subsequently seen him wearing since, the rattle of keys in the lock got me swinging around. My fists readied, only to drop as Kyle entered the apartment carrying two large paper sacks.

His grin was immediate and brought with it the attraction that, up to now, I'd pushed into the far recesses of my mind... *kind of.*

My gaze skimmed over him, and my gut tightened for a different reason. Today's outfit was a slim-fitting pair of pants and a fitted button-down in dark gray. He'd styled his hair off his face. Honestly, I much preferred the scruffier style he'd originally had.

"I couldn't remember what I'd left in the freezer, so I dropped by the store to grab some stuff." He kicked the door closed behind him, his black boot connecting with the wood loudly as his smile dipped. "Everything okay? Is Calliope all right?" He glanced at the couch and the TV, the pictures flickering soundlessly.

"Calliope's in her room...your spare room," I corrected quickly. Killer would be back the next day, and I was sure Kyle would want us out of his hair. I had enough cash to rent a motel room for a couple of weeks. After that, I'd have to see.

At the counter, Kyle plonked the bags down, then glanced at me, his brows knotting. "It's her room for as long as she wants and needs it. The same goes for you. Linc will be back tomorrow, but it's gonna take time to figure out what you need." His attention returned to the bags, and he emptied them onto the countertop. "You had any supper yet? I'm starvin'."

Not exactly sure how to address the offer he'd just made, I walked over to him. Although I didn't get too close and give in to the temptation to inhale his crisp scent. "Not yet."

Chapter Six

Kyle

I cursed under my breath at the stony expression and quick overcorrection about the status of my spare room being Calliope's. My smile slipped as I tried to figure out how to get Conall to accept my help. Yep, I was being selfish again because I wanted a chance to get to know him. Something about Conall made it impossible to ignore him or my reaction to him. The attraction sizzled between us in the limited time I'd spent in his company. Especially when he wasn't being all stony-faced like he was now. I was positive it wasn't one-sided. I just needed to figure out how to get him to let down his walls.

His first thoughts were always about his sister, as they should be, but that didn't mean he didn't have a boyfriend in Round Rock. So far, he'd limited any personal information about himself, and I hadn't figured out a way to change it without making it obvious I was interested in him.

The distance Conall kept between us was noticeable when his neck stretched to its limit, so he could get a better look at the stuff I'd emptied onto the counter.

"You interested in me cooking something for you and your sister?" I once more upped the wattage of my smile, hoping he wouldn't tell me to take a hike.

Dark brows knitted together as his gaze moved to me. "What you got in mind?" Something was off. His tone held no inflection. And now that I was really looking at him, I noticed a tension about him I hadn't seen since I'd opened the door to him at Linc's place. It hadn't been there the day before when I'd checked in to see if they were comfortable and had everything they needed. So what had caused it? Had he gotten word about the guy who he'd attacked? It had taken Nutty telling me in no uncertain terms that I wasn't to interfere and reach out to Rattlesnake before we'd spoken to Linc to keep my cell phone in my pocket.

River had been as good as gold and not mentioned our late-night callers when she'd spoken to him.

His head tilted, and I realized I hadn't responded. "Burgers. I make a mean chili burger. You interested?"

He licked his lips, and I watched the move, attempting not to think too hard about what his lips would feel like against mine. What would he taste like?

"Yeah, okay. No one can fuck up a chili burger." There was a hint of playfulness and the first glimpse of a smile.

Motherfucker!

Swallowing became hard as I imagined how gorgeous he'd look wearing a full smile. The attraction whizzing through me went up another notch, and this time it took genuine effort to ignore the stirring in my lower belly.

"I'll check with Calli. See if she wants a chili burger." He walked off around the counter.

My gaze lowered to Conall's ass as it flexed in the well-fitting denim I'd found in the back of Linc's closet. I'd also grabbed a couple of Linc's T-shirts, as he was more Conall's size than me. I'd had limited options because I hadn't wanted to go out to buy clothes in Belton with the gossips. The last thing we needed was Sid asking questions. Up to now, I'd avoided my brothers to keep things on the down-low. Even Ali and Troy were giving me the side-eye. I'd be glad when Linc got back the next day. This was worse than trying to keep a secret from my mom.

Once Conall was out of sight, I breathed in and rubbed at my face. *Get a grip!*

After a glance at the food, I pulled out the things I'd need to make the chili topping for the burger. I was preparing the chili and had the burgers on the grill when Conall reappeared.

Keeping it friendly, I nodded toward the refrigerator. "Can you grab me a beer?"

His reply was to grab a bottle, pop the lid, and leave it on the counter. I eyed him as I stirred the pot, scenting the room with spice. "You don't want one?"

"I didn't want to be rude and assume. You've already done a lot for us. I don't like owing anyone," he replied stiffly.

Oh!

Picking up the beer bottle and taking a sip, I eyed him, considering how to phrase what I wanted to say. His gaze revealed none of what he was thinking. "Do you want a beer?"

The sigh was low, but I heard it. "Yeah."

"Then have one. I invited you to stay and make yourselves at home." I gave him a pointed look. "I meant it."

"Thanks." He hesitated as if he was going to say more, then lifted his chin and walked to get a beer.

The silence between us crackled, and I wasn't sure if it was all tension or attraction. I wanted it to be the latter. "Heard anything from Dog?"

His whole body tensed and the beer bottle he held stopped mid-air. "No...did you reach out to Rattlesnake? He called me."

The accusing tone didn't miss its target. After dropping the spoon in the pot, I bristled and twisted to face him. "No," I snapped angrily. I lowered the beer bottle to the counter and stomped to Conall, poking him in the chest in a temper. "I said I'd help. And yeah, I mentioned Rattlesnake, but I don't do the dirty behind a brother's back. It ain't my style."

He took the hand I'd poked him with in a firm grip, his gaze sizzling hotter than the meat on the grill spitting and hissing behind us. His gaze focused on my lips, and my breath shuddered out of my chest at the desire he didn't hide. There was no time to celebrate that I'd been right before his mouth crushed against mine.

The hand holding mine turned into a demanding grip as his mouth punished mine in a hungry kiss. It was almost like he'd been in a desert and was taking a drink for the first time in weeks, months... fuck, years. My lips parted at the demand, allowing his tongue to slide into my mouth, tasting. His hand trapped mine against his chest as he tugged me against him fully. The scent of my soap and his musk were a heady combination with the hard wall of muscle that pinned me to the counter. The ledge dug into my back.

When had we moved?

It didn't matter when his groin pressed against mine, hardness meeting hardness. He ground against me, and my free hand went to his ass to pull him closer.

The sound of glass hitting tile pulled me from my sex-induced stupor. Chest heaving, my eyes tried to focus. My mouth felt swollen and abused in the best possible way.

"Con...erm...are we having supper?" Calliope stuttered from behind me, and my face flamed at what she might have seen.

Conall grunted and released me, his flushed face revealing nothing of what was happening in his head. When he bent, I noticed the wet floor and broken glass. It took four more seconds to register he must have dropped his beer bottle and that the lower part of my left leg was wet.

That was some fucking kiss!

The scent of the meat got me moving without looking in Calliope's direction. I worked on pretending we hadn't just been caught making out in my kitchen. Or that my cock tried to make a run for it through the zipper of my pants like a running back wanting to make the winning score. It was tough to act normal with Conall cleaning up the floor and at crotch level, with the ability to see his effect on me.

"This isn't awkward much," Calliope muttered.

Working on seeing the funny side of it as my cock continued to throb painfully against the fly of my pants, I fired her a sheepish grin. "You wanna try being the one who got caught making out?"

She giggled with abandon. It was great to hear after what she'd been through. "It's the first time I've seen Con get his move on."

"Shut up, Calli."

"You might wanna put the beer bottle down next time. Not sure covering the guy you're with in beer is a good thing...unless he was na—"

Conall shot up so fast his hair flew around his face, and I bit my lip to stop from laughing at his wide eyes and pale cheeks. "What...you stop that!" he choked out.

She shrugged as she sat at the table, her grin wide and unrepentant. If she didn't have two black eyes marring her beautiful face, I could have made myself believe the situation was different and Conall was here because he wanted to be.

They continued to bicker back and forth as I finished making the burgers, grinning while listening to them.

When everything was ready, Conall set plates on the counter after cleaning up the mess. He didn't once meet my gaze as I attempted several times to smile at him and show I was more than happy with what had happened—besides the beer dropping and getting caught by his little sister.

At the table, the three of us tucked into the food. Conall's gaze remained on his plate the entire time, and I swallowed a sigh of frustration. One of many when I contemplated my list of unresolved issues with the infuriating man opposite me.

Chapter Seven

Conall

Under cover of darkness, I headed toward Killer's home. I'd left my motorcycle in Killer's garage, and I didn't want to waste my cash on a rideshare or bus, so walking it was. Calliope wanted to come, but she—in my opinion—wasn't up for the trek. And the bruising would draw unwanted attention. Also, if there was going to be an issue with Killer, I didn't want her in the line of fire.

Liz, pleased with how Calliope was doing, gave me a card for a counselor, which was in my jacket pocket. Liz had also gotten her friend to print off all the test results so I could give them to Mason. I wasn't sure of the costs. Lawyers and counseling wouldn't be cheap, but Calliope deserved the best, and I'd do anything to get it for her. It was my damn fault we were in this mess because I hadn't dealt with Earl earlier. Not that I'd suspected the fucker would...

Bile burned the back of my throat, and I closed my eyes briefly to shut out the scene that liked to play over in my mind, reminding me that I'd failed Calliope.

I growled at the empty street, crossing over, shoulders hunched.

Life fucking sucked.

Keeping my thoughts under control took effort with the stress of the unknown outcome of the evening. There were too many things that could go wrong, and being told to fuck off was at the bottom of the worry list.

When I approached Killer's place, all my emotions I'd locked down tight. Years of practice helped. Lights glowed in every window as I stared up at the house. My first thought was not seeing Killer, but seeing Kyle.

The man was... I ran a hand through my messy hair and groaned at the fact he was too good for the likes of me.

Why had I given in?

My lips had buzzed for hours after the kiss. I wanted to drink him in until I was drowning in him. Once I'd gotten a taste, fuck, it was nothing like I'd suspected it would be. Or dreamed. He was all neat and put together, but he kissed hard and dirty. Matching me until I'd lost my sanity and forgot I was holding the damn beer in my desperation to touch him.

The warmth of the evening air didn't compete with the heat of embarrassment that came with how close I'd been to tearing off his clothes and fucking him right there on the kitchen counter. If I hadn't dropped the bottle and smashed it, I was positive Calliope would have got more of a show.

Acting like I was unaffected during the meal was possibly one of the hardest things to do. I'd tasted none of the food and taken Calliope's word that it was good. I'd thanked him, helped clean up, and then all but shoved him out the door of his own home before Calliope took it upon herself to leave me alone with him again. The desire between us was potent and lethal, even if taken in small quantities. It would be a mistake to act on it.

Really!

The sarcastic voice was all Calliope, who'd made several pointed comments today about how nice Kyle was. I didn't need her reminding me when we were living in his damn apartment and eating his food.

Blowing out a big breath, I glanced about, giving myself time to divert my thoughts from Kyle. The inky black sky held multiple stars. The air was warm and smelled of spring. Kyle lived in a nice part of the city. Mostly apartments with no yards. It wasn't something to complain about, given where I'd come from. Outside the trailers, piles of stinky trash and old broken furniture added to the awfulness of the place. Killer's place was something else. It was a home the likes of me could only dream about owning.

The cell phone in my back pocket buzzed, and I slipped my hand in and saw Kyle's name on the screen. When I opened the message and read it, I shook my head.

Stop admiring the garden and get in here!

I glanced from the screen to the house. There, on the third floor in the window, was Kyle. I couldn't see his expression, but I suspected he was grinning. The heat in my face increased, and I hoped the streetlights didn't reveal my embarrassment at getting caught hovering like a dork.

With my phone back in my pocket, I'd barely pressed the bell before the door opened. Expecting Kyle, I eyed Killer warily as his gaze swept over me from head to toe. Sure, he hadn't missed that I was wearing his clothes. I worked to keep still and meet his hard stare.

Long dark hair hung around his face, landing on powerful shoulders. Dressed in dark jeans and a black T-shirt, he looked exactly as he had the last time I'd seen him: scary as fuck.

"Killer." I nodded, suspecting Kyle had already filled him in when he didn't appear surprised to see me.

"Poppy, where you at?" River's voice floated from somewhere inside.

"Come in." His dark brows knotted as he stepped back. "Stay at the door," he called back over his shoulder.

River appeared a second later at the top of the stairs. Her ponytail was lopsided, and there were stains on the sunny yellow top that matched her leggings. She grinned at me. "Con, where is Calli? Is she not feeling good?" she asked, continuing down the stairs toward us, her gaze searching the hallway.

A smile spread over my lips at her genuine concern. "She's at Kyle's place."

Killer lifted River into his arms and settled her on his hip. His expression softened and weirded me out. The two sides of him were hard to marry. The doting father versus the president of a motorcycle chapter that was infamous around these parts for being one tough motherfucker.

"Weren't you supposed to be upstairs getting ready for bed?" he asked, the frustration clear in his tone.

"Poppy, I missed ya." She rubbed her cheek against Killer's unshaven jaw and giggled. "And it's polite to say hello to guests, Daddy said."

"Did I hear my name being used in vain?" Mason wore casual clothes. Pressed slacks and a button-down, no suit today, but he still looked every inch the lawyer he was when he appeared from the back of the house.

Mason and Killer were opposites, yet they worked. The way Killer looked at Mason and Mason stared back could blister paintwork, which weirded me out once more.

"What is it with you pair? I told you both I wanted to talk to Conall alone." The growl lacked any proper bite.

Mason stroked a hand over River's head and winked at her. "From what Kyle has mentioned, I need to be here for the conversation. I know I mentioned it to you. Has our five-day vacation given you memory problems?"

His tone was firm and one I suspected few argued with. The flex of Killer's jaw suggested he was about to when there was the sound of boots on wood. Killer growled and swung to see who was on the stairs.

Kyle stopped mid-step, his expression one of apprehension with the grooves deepening at the sides of his mouth. His gaze met mine over everyone's heads with what appeared to be an apology in his eyes. "Hey."

Killer glanced from Kyle to me, his gaze narrowing before it returned to Kyle. "As it appears no fu...anyone," he added at the last moment when River aimed a hard stare at him that rivaled his, "is listenin' to me. Let's take this upstairs. I need a beer." Killer didn't wait for anyone to respond, heading for the stairs.

Kyle swung around and gave me a view of his ass. I glanced away quickly when it tempted me to stare at the bubble butt that bounced when he walked.

Mason chuckled and gave me a friendly slap on the shoulder. "It's good to see you, Conall." His smile disappeared. "I'm just sorry it's under these circumstances."

It was pointless responding. He was right. The circumstances were shitty. The only question I wanted to waste breath on was: were they going to help me?

In the living room, I took the seat offered and collected my thoughts while everyone got organized with drinks. I took the beer bottle from Killer and nodded my thanks. I didn't look in Kyle's direction when he took the seat off to my left, a bottle dangling from his fingers, reminding me of the day before. Not that I could forget!

Nutty entered the room dressed in a short black dress, her face made up. Dark smoky eyes and bright-red lips went with the spiked-up hair and killer heels. "There you are, missy. It's bedtime."

"Poppy and Daddy only just got home."

At the light of defiance in her eyes, I clamped my lips together to stop from smiling, so used to this behavior.

Nutty's hands went to her slim hips, and her head tilted to the side, her hair unmoving. "Linc and Mason got home three hours ago and you've chewed their ears off ever since."

"It's Friday. I don't got school tomorrow," she argued back.

"And it's half an hour past your Friday bedtime. Up and wiggle that butt into the bedroom," Nutty said firmly.

There was a little more complaining, but five minutes later, after several hugs and kisses, she disappeared with Nutty.

Once the living room door shut behind her, Killer looked at me. "Talk."

Blunt, as usual. It helped to settle the flies buzzing like crazy in my stomach as I laid out the events of the night. Still wearing my jacket, I tugged out the test result paperwork and handed it to Mason, sweating bullets when he took it but remained silent.

"What's Dog got to say?"

Killer eyed me in a way that left me uncertain about his thoughts when I answered, "He's not spoken to me. I messaged and told him Earl had raped Calliope. All I've had is radio silence ever since." I didn't let on about Rattlesnake.

"You don't know what condition Earl is in? If he's dead or alive?" Mason questioned, his gaze on the papers he held, his voice distracted.

I cursed and debated how to avoid dropping Rattlesnake into this mess.

Killer came forward in his seat, hard eyes pinning me in place. "If you want our help, don't fucking think about lying."

"Rattlesnake reached out to him," Kyle answered before I could find my tongue due to Killer's sharp tone that could cut metal. "Con doesn't want to cause a problem for Rattlesnake."

"I can speak for myself," I snapped, then regretted it when a look of hurt flashed in his eyes before they hooded and he glanced down.

"Then speak!" Killer snapped angrily. "If you're bringing trouble to my door, I want to know the ins and outs of your fucking asshole before I put my brothers at risk."

Mason chuckled, but the stare he aimed at Killer was dark and dangerous. "The only asshole you'll know the ins and outs of is mine, just for the record." He twisted in my direction. "Talk me through what you know about Earl's condition."

"He's breathing with a tube down his throat. He's not woken up yet."

Whatever emotions Mason felt at that weren't evident when he nodded and glanced at my bruised hands. "Chances of survival?"

I shrugged. "He was breathin' when I stopped. His face looked like smashed pizza."

Another nod. "Do you have pictures of Calliope's injuries?"

The clinical way he asked helped when I took out my cell phone and opened the message Liz had sent with all the attachments. Ones I hadn't looked at. "Nutty's nurse friend took these."

Killer moved to see the phone screen, and I looked away. Kyle became my focus as he got up silently, walked over to perch his ass on the couch arm, and rested a hand on my shoulder. The weight and his cologne's fresh scent as his body leaned into me were enough to give me something to pay attention to. For reasons I didn't want to examine too closely, I stayed put, working to keep my breathing under control.

When Killer glanced up, my chest tightened at the fierce anger flashing in his eyes. It was unmistakable. I'd seen it myself in the mirror every time I thought about that night.

"You have enough evidence here to put Earl in prison for sure," Mason said with a tightness to his voice that hadn't been there initially. "Problem is, no one likes a person who makes himself judge and jury."

I was up off the seat, nearly knocking Kyle to the floor. "He'd beaten her and was fucking raping her," I shouted, then reined it back at Killer's look. "He violated my little sister! She ain't ever gonna forget what that slime ball did to her. She's the one who's gotta live with that. What he got, he fucking deserved."

Mason stood and stepped in front of me. "I agree with you."

Those four words were a splash of icy water, and I sagged back on the couch, the anger draining away. "Then help me...please," I begged.

Chapter Eight

Kyle

The early appointment I had booked for seven-thirty—the dude had to be at work at nine—got my ass out of bed far too soon for my liking. Deciding to walk off the sleepless night from knowing Conall was in the room next to mine, I headed out the door with an insulated cup of coffee.

I'd left the pot on the stove and pancakes warming in the oven with a note saying when I'd be home later. It was weird having people in my place, especially when one of them took up most of my thoughts. My parents and brother had come once for the holidays and stayed for three days. This was different.

A part of me wanted the level of intimacy of having a man I was interested in at my place. Another part suggested I was running before I could walk the length of myself when there was little to write home about between Conall and me. I was hard-pressed to call it anything. Even a friendship with Conall gave mixed messages. It also didn't feel like it was because of his sister. Was it something I had done?

Was it the kiss? Yeah, I might have pushed his buttons, and I hadn't held back. The attraction on my part was off the charts. If there was such a thing to measure how I felt when he kissed me. The man's mouth was a lethal weapon when he used it to wipe away all coherent thoughts.

While lying awake listening out for sounds the night before, I'd run through what had happened at Linc's. For the first time, Conall had let down the wall that was there to protect him from whatever life had thrown at him. My bet was a lot. I was convinced he didn't often beg, judging by how he'd done it last night with Linc. There'd been a visible change in him when he'd begged.

I sipped at the coffee and tried to figure out what came next. I wanted to show Conall I was interested in more. Yet, how to do that without being classed as an insensitive jerk? Calliope needed help, and I'd wanted to give it regardless of who her brother was. That had to count for something, right?

Birds chirped, and the bright-blue sky didn't add much pep to my step when I ran through options and discarded each one. Dating and I had been on hiatus since Preppy Boy back in Rock Springs, and I'd somehow gotten myself into a rut. One that got deeper with every attempt I made to make myself a little hipper. Or was it trendy? Who the fuck knew?

What did I know? Fuck-all worked.

A pair of green-gray eyes flashed into my head like they did every time I'd worked myself up to chatting a guy up. And yeah, recently, I'd compared every dude to Conall. One eye fuck, and I'd been fucked royally. Now he was here, sleeping under my roof. What was I going to do about it?

Down the street from Linc's, I spotted a motorcycle I was unfamiliar with at the curbside. I glanced at my watch, speeding up. Being a member of Dark Angels, I knew all the local motorcycles affiliated with the club. The one at the curbside wasn't local.

Was my seven-thirty appointment here early, and had Danny switched his motorcycle?

I pushed at the door, expecting it to be open but found it locked. The frown deepened as I dug into my pocket with my free hand and pulled out my keys. Door open, and the alarm disengaged, I glanced around. There was nothing out of the ordinary. The reception desk was clean, as was the waiting area, yet I got a sense of unease in the pit of my stomach.

Who owned the motorcycle outside? Was this connected to Conall?

Listening for any noise, I tilted my head as I walked toward the stairs leading up to the first floor, treading lightly. Halfway up the second flight of stairs, I heard an unfamiliar voice. Not one to poke my nose into anyone's business. I hesitated.

The deep timbre of the voice was familiar, and the air in my lungs decided I didn't need it when I calculated what time Linc must have called Dog for him to be here just after seven in the morning.

I went into my room, placed the coffee cup down on the built-in counter that housed all my equipment, and walked back out, ready for whatever was needed. In Dark Angels, I'd learned how to kick ass and stand up for my family.

Conall isn't your family!

Ignoring the snippy internal voice pointing out the obvious, I went up the stairs silently. The bees having a party in my gut didn't stop me from wanting to add my two cents' worth to this shit show. Calliope was a sweet girl, and Conall...

Dog's voice got louder. "You should have sent him straight back, not fucking summoning me like some fucking genie in a lamp. I don't do your bidding, Killer."

"Sit your ass back down. I ain't after fuck-all except answers. And I wasn't here to send him back."

"Not that we'd have done that," Mason stated in a no-nonsense way I'd classified as his lawyer voice.

There was a pause before Linc continued, "Why the fuck have you not been in touch with Conall? A member of Chosen Few brutally raped his fucking sister. What Conall did was defend his sister, something commendable, not something to fucking ostracize him from the club without giving him a chance to explain." The pain in Linc's voice was unmistakable and tugged at memories of our recent house cleaning.

Furious didn't even come close to how Linc reacted to being set up for rape. He'd upped and changed much about Dark

Angels to protect his sister's daughter. The man was all about protecting family. I hadn't doubted Linc would help, even when we'd left last night with no definitive plan for Conall and his sister.

It would seem Linc had a plan all along and kept it close to his chest.

Didn't he trust me?

"You need to keep it down. River is just down the hallway, sleeping," Mason stated calmly but firmly.

I stood at the top of the stairs, undecided about revealing I was there when it seemed Linc thought he'd be alone when he'd called this early-morning meeting.

"It's club business Linc. You know I ain't gonna discuss that with you. Earl is—"

"A fucking scumbag!" Linc supplied furiously. The look on his face last night when he'd gone through the pictures Liz had taken of Calliope's injuries spoke to the truth of what Linc was saying.

Before I realized my intention, I stepped into the kitchen. "Linc, Mason, everything okay up here?"

Three sets of eyes aimed stares at me. A lesser man might have turned tail and run back out.

"What are you doin' here so early?" Linc demanded angrily. The temper was clearly still riding him.

I couldn't tear my gaze away from Dog, who sat silently with a challenging stare that equaled Linc's. "I've... erm... an early appointment." I nodded at the man sitting next to Mason. "Dog, good to see you."

Dog's eyes glittered as he gave me the up-down and nodded slowly. "Kyle."

"Kyle, Kyle, you up there?" Danny called loudly, breaking the moment of tension.

"Go on. I'll catch you later." Lincoln's tone was not one to be argued with.

With a nod and one last look at Dog, I left. Downstairs, I offered Danny a smile I wasn't feeling.

He didn't seem to notice as he talked excitedly. "Man, I can't wait to see how the 3-D effect on the dragon's claws turns out." The full sleeve on his right arm was almost complete. The dragon's lower body and claws were the last part. He wanted them holding on to the demon I'd done six weeks earlier. This was the last session. It had taken six months and every spare bit of cash Danny had to get to this point. His girlfriend wasn't as impressed as he was.

It didn't take long to get Danny settled on the chair, his eyes closed as he mostly dosed. He was one of those folks who wasn't bothered by the pain. The buzz of the gun was the only sound in the room. I'd left my music off, wanting to hear if anything went down above me. The lack of shouts or thudding did nothing to calm my two-stepping nerves.

An hour later, I heard the heavy tread of boots on the stairs. The urge to stop and see Linc battled the need to be professional and finish the tattoo. Danny stirred and glanced down at the arm I'd been working on. "Fuck, I wasn't sure you'd be as good as Linc, but man, that's one badass tattoo."

I didn't take offense. Linc was a master at tattooing. I wore many of his pieces. "Thanks," I muttered, working on finishing inking the last of the claws. Then I sat back, looking at different angles to check it was perfect.

A slow smile spread over my lips. "I think this is my best piece to date."

Danny's grin matched mine. "It's fucking awesome. I love it." He lifted his arm and looked at it. The blood and redness didn't take away from the overall effect. "I think I'll need to match up my other arm."

I laughed at him, shaking my head. "You aiming for being single?"

"Nah, she loves me. I can sweet talk her." Danny sat patiently while I cleaned his skin and wrapped it up.

I chuckled at his faith because he'd moaned like a fucker last time over how crazy his girlfriend got at the amount he'd paid versus what he'd spent on a birthday gift for her.

When finished, I handed over the care instruction sheet. He wasn't a novice at getting a tattoo, but it never harmed to reiterate what was needed to protect the tattoo. Like all artwork, it needed to be kept out of direct sunlight. Or in this case, sunscreen used once healed.

"Nutty should be available to take payment." I paused, giving him a toothy grin. "And book another appointment for you." I knew full well he wouldn't be able to resist getting the other arm done. One was never enough.

"You're evil, dude, encouraging me like that." His gaze went to the wall of artwork I had. "Think you could come up with something unusual for the other arm?"

"Yup, you got anything you're particularly interested in?" I continued to clean up while he walked over to get a closer look at my designs. The art degree I had made the design part real fun. First, it came down to body parts, then once I'd figured out angles and creases, I got creative. Then came the fun: inking a person with my artwork. I never grew tired of it.

"Nah, I think I'd like to see what you can come up with."

Blood warming at the challenge, I nodded at him when he faced me. "Can do. I'll work on it over the next few weeks. Book in with Nutty for a month's time, and we can look at what I've come up with, see if you're interested." Even if he didn't want the design, I'd put it on my Instagram for prospective clients.

"Cool, and thanks." He waved his now-covered arm, heading for the door.

"Don't forget to send me a picture when it's healed for my wall."

"Will do. See ya." He disappeared out the door, and I finished up.

I popped my head out the door, listening for sounds coming from next door. At the lack of voices and the buzzing of a tattoo gun, I headed into Linc's room. He had his back to me and was staring outside.

"You got a couple of minutes?" I asked, already closing the door behind me. Linc was a hard one to read, and sometimes I needed to remind myself there was a line between us and club business. One I was about to cross.

He didn't turn. "I didn't mention reaching out to Dog 'cause I wasn't sure he'd come. And I wanted to hear what he had to say."

The steely edge to his voice was a warning I heeded, and I worked to hold back my anger when he answered my unspoken question. I didn't know if my anger was justified after what little I'd heard this morning, so I worked on keeping it out of my voice. "And? Did he explain why he left one member hanging in the breeze by his damn balls for protecting his sister from a *rapist*?" Maybe not as calm as I wanted.

When Linc turned, he aimed a look at me that could have melted metal. The air got stuck in my lungs, but I didn't back down. Conall had a right to be protected, and Earl did not. It was as simple as that.

"The cops have been all over their asses. Someone could monitor any communication with Conall, hence the silence. Dog's worried. If Earl wakes up and blabs, the club will come under closer scrutiny. If he dies? Same thing. So it's a shit show whichever way you look at it."

"Do you blame Conall for doing what he did?"

I'd seen Linc mad, but the icy stare was utterly terrifying. "If anyone touched River in the way Calliope was, I wouldn't stop until he breathed his last. There would be no place on this earth they'd be safe."

Okay, that answered my question. "What are we gonna do to protect them? Is Mason gonna help?"

Linc ran a hand through his hair, glancing at the closed door. "Mason was a yes to helping the second Conall showed him the pictures. The only problem is, will he be defending someone from life in prison or putting a scumbag away?"

Chapter Nine

Conall

Met with the scent of coffee and pancakes as I came out of my bedroom, I groaned and rubbed at my gurgling stomach. I'd been too fucked in the head last night to eat and was ready for what I could smell. A fluttering came at thoughts of seeing Kyle after we'd parted last night with an awkwardness I hadn't known how to deal with.

I stopped in the living room as my gaze swept the empty kitchen. I realized he'd left as I eyed the coffeepot. I checked my watch. It was barely after eight. Did he leave early to avoid talking? What time did they open the shop? Was it eight? Or did he not feel comfortable with me being in his space?

Second-guessing myself wasn't a habit, so I shut down the questions and followed my nose to the coffeepot. I checked the oven and found a covered dish full of pancakes.

"That smells good. You gonna share?" Calliope asked as she trailed into the kitchen wearing shorts and a baggy T-shirt that fell off one shoulder as she came over to nudge me with her elbow.

Placing the dish down on the stove, I nodded. "Get the plates and cups. There's maple syrup in the cupboard if you want it." She had a sweet tooth that she liked to indulge in when the chance arose.

"Great." Bare feet slapped on the floor as she moved easily about the kitchen.

She looked at ease, but I didn't miss the tightness around her lips or the rounded shoulders.

She'd been in bed when we'd gotten home last night. There'd been no debate whether I'd wake her that late to talk. With everything up in the air, we hadn't seriously talked about what came next. Kyle was insistent we could stay at his place until...whatever happened. It was the "whatever" that worried me. Calliope wasn't of legal age to go off on her own. We had no close family other than distant cousins we hadn't seen in over a decade. They hadn't come to Mom's funeral, so there was no way they'd be interested in taking care of Calli.

Would the court trust a fourteen-year-old girl with her twenty-six-year-old brother who was part of a motorcycle chapter with a bad rep? Or one who was up for possible homicide? I swallowed the bitter laughter at the definite no to all those questions. Stomach twisting into painful knots, my appetite deserted me at how that left us up a creek without a fucking paddle.

A shiver of unease ran down my spine at the realization that I wouldn't be able to fight my way out of trouble this time.

"You gonna just grind your teeth or serve those pancakes?" The question came with uncertainty and a wary expression no fourteen-year-old should wear.

I grabbed the plates she'd laid on the counter and filled them. I forced myself to appear like I was hungry. "You back to giving sass?"

She took the plate from me and placed it next to the coffee cups she'd filled when I wasn't paying attention. "Yup, you need me to keep you on your toes." It lacked any real Calliope spirit.

I sat down next to her and nudged her shoulder with mine. "You've done that since you surprised us with an early Christmas gift."

She giggled, and the sound lightened the mood, if only for a few seconds.

Silence fell as we both ate and pretended that the weight of the world wasn't hanging around our shoulders.

Pushing the pancakes around the plate for the fifth time, Calliope laid a hand on the one holding the fork. "You gonna tell me what happened with Killer and his boyfriend, the lawyer? They gonna help us?"

The bravery left me dry-mouthed and proud. I glanced sideways at her. "Mason is gonna do some digging on Earl first, see how bad he is, then he wants to meet with you to talk—"

"About what he did." She squeezed my hand. "It's okay, Con. I'll talk to him if it stops you goin' to jail."

I dropped the fork and turned my hand over, interlinking our fingers, twisting on the seat to look fully at her. "You're so fucking brave."

Her eyes glistened as she shook her head. "No, I just wanna be able to sleep at night knowing he can't...touch me again."

"Ah fuck," I ground out and let go of her hand to lift her like I did when she was little. I carried her to the couch and cuddled her as she wept into my chest. Life hadn't been a bed of fucking roses, but my life had gotten better after she was born. She'd looked up to me, and when life had gone to hell in a handcart, instead of heading into the darkness, I'd used her lightness to keep going.

She had an inner strength she said came from me, and I held her now, letting her take whatever she needed. Until now, she hadn't really had a crying jag, so I rubbed at her back, feeling useless, furious, and the worst kind of brother for not seeing Earl's intentions. All the while, I uttered stupid shit until Calliope's raw sobs turned to whimpers and sniffling. Unsure how long we sat on the couch, a knock at the door interrupted us.

Her head rose off my shoulder. My T-shirt was wet and stuck to my skin as she glanced at the door, rubbing at her tear-stained cheeks. The next knock was louder than the first. Up to now, the only person who'd been on the other side of the door was Kyle. The next knock painfully twisted the knots in my belly.

Calliope slipped off my lap, and I got up, the both of us silent as I went to the door. Taking a deep breath, already suspecting who might be on the other side, I opened the door.

The massively built guy standing with his hand raised as if he was going to knock again met my stare with one that shielded his thoughts. "Hey, Runner." Dog's tone also gave nothing away.

"Dog, whassup?"

Calliope's lips parted, and I shook my head, giving her a warning look. She nodded and bit her knuckle, a habit she'd had since she was little, to stop herself from talking as Dog stepped fully into the room.

He glanced about, his gaze lingering on Calliope, who he nodded at. "Calli."

"Dog," she mumbled, her hand dropping to her side. Her gaze dipped to the carpet as she remained standing.

Shutting the door, I remained silent, unsure what to think about Dog's arrival. Only a few people knew where I was, so it didn't take a genius to figure out who had told him we were here.

Dog stopped in the middle of the living space, his wide shoulders stiff under his leather jacket. "You should have come to me if you were having issues with Earl."

Bristling under the hard stare, my back molars ground together to keep control of what wanted to fire out of my mouth.

"I didn't tell Con how bad it was getting." Calliope's voice quivered as she stood straight, meeting Dog's stare. "I thought I could handle it. The occasional hand on my ass. A brush that touched my chest. It wasn't so bad, especially with him at the clubhouse more." Her slim shoulders rose and fell. "But when he drank…" Her gaze was pleading when she glanced at me.

"Ahh fuck, Calli! Why didn't you tell me?" I ignored Dog and went to my sister, taking her hands. "I would have done something."

A flush rode over her blotchy cheeks. Her hands squeezed mine, her eyes begging me to understand. "I know. I thought this time I could handle it. Stop running to you to get you to shoulder my problems as well as your own. I saw how he ragged on your ass all the time, not giving you a minute's peace. No one seemed to care about that, so I kept quiet." She aimed the latter at Dog.

A mean growl got me glancing at him. "What? Would you have done something? He was your friend and brother." The accusation was there, but I could do little about it when the evidence of what Earl was capable of was in front of us.

"I'd have had a word with him, Runner."

Years of frustration bubbled over, and I let go of Calliope and spun to face Dog. I didn't care that this could get my ass handed to me. I'd been spoiling for a fight since Calliope had stopped me from killing the son-of-a-bitch. "Like the other times that I came to you. What did you say?" I tapped my lower lip. "Oh yeah, '*grow a pair, Runner, and remember you're a fucking member of Chosen Few.*' Wasn't that how it went? I can take my fucking lumps like the best of them."

I jabbed a finger in Calliope's direction. "This is way fucking more than that." The hard edge to my tone brought a warning light into Dog's eyes. I was past caring. "Have the brothers met to discuss what happens to Earl? Or was that meeting about me?"

An ugly red coated Dog's cheeks. His lips tightened.

"Yeah, thought so. Judged before you even gave a brother a chance to have his say. I'm done. You, the fucking brothers, I'm not a fucking second-class citizen, Dog, and my sister surely ain't." I walked to the door.

Hand on the doorknob, I stopped when Dog touched my arm. "Earl looks like a piece of ground beef. There was no sign of you, no word. What was I supposed to think when Earl's wallet was gone after payday? You and Calliope had skipped out, leaving a mess for us to clean up."

Calliope sobbed, and I swallowed the burning bile. "Someone called the cops. Do you think it would've been sensible to come to the clubhouse with my sister? To show off what Earl had done just to prove I was innocent?" I let go of the door, shook off Dog's hand, and went to get my phone.

A photo on the screen, I shoved it in Dog's face. He winced, and there looked to be sympathy in his gaze, but it was too late. I was done. "This right here is what *your best friend is capable of*," I spat angrily, my hand shaking as it dropped to my side. "My thoughts were about protecting her. Keeping her safe!

That's not your concern, is it?" I shook my head, answering for him. "It's time you left. My patched jacket is still at the clubhouse. You're welcome to give it to whoever. Now get the fuck out!"

Dog stiffened, his gaze as unwavering as mine. "You're making a mistake."

I held up my hand to stop him from saying more. I didn't want to hear it. "Maybe I am. But a brother who decides without all the facts 'cause of who he's friends with ain't a brother who has my back. So how am I supposed to trust you?" I shook my head again, my energy waning at thoughts of an uncertain future.

Dog walked past me, his back rigid. He stopped in the doorway and looked back over his shoulder with what appeared to be regret. "You know where I am if you change your mind." On that, he left, the door closing quietly. The latch snicking was the only noise before Calliope began sobbing earnestly.

"Calli, it'll be fine, I swear," I muttered, going to her.

With one arm over her shoulder, I answered my ringing phone. My brows rose as I pressed the accept icon and put the phone to my ear after seeing the name on the screen. Tense, my fingers gripped the phone hard enough to make the outer casing crack. "Kyle."

"Dog's been here—"

"Has he?" I growled.

"Yeah. Linc called him last night. He came early this morning. Can you come to the shop and bring Calliope?" His voice was hushed.

What the fuck was going on? I eyed Calliope's healing face, puffy eyes, and blotchy cheeks. The faded bruising and healing cuts were clear enough to get folks looking at her. "I thought we were supposed to be keeping a low profile." I said the first thing that came to mind when I wasn't sure where this was leading.

"Shit...I think Nutty put some makeup in the bag of stuff she gave to Calliope. I got a baseball cap in the closet in the hallway. She could pull it down low over her face. Linc and Mason wanna talk to both of you. *It's important*."

Bile hit the back of my throat as my mind raced at all the possibilities. None of them boded well for Calliope and me. There was fuck-all I could do now, and with nowhere left to run, what options did I have? "What time do we need to be there?"

Chapter Ten

Kyle

Linc hadn't said anything about whether Dog had asked where Conall was staying, and since my next client had arrived, I'd had no time to continue the conversation with him to ask. River had seen to that when she'd come in looking for Linc to help her get ready for a planned sleepover at her best friend's, Luna, house. She'd left half an hour ago, right before Conall arrived. I'd been eavesdropping, so sue me.

It was impossible to concentrate. Conall was above me with Calliope. After my talk with Linc, I'd been the one to suggest calling Conall and getting him to come over to the shop. It was Saturday, and Mason was home, so keeping a low profile was easier, except for getting them through the shop. The level of uncertainty with everything made it worth the risk. Conall hadn't sounded as convinced as me. But with the possibility of Dog now knowing where Conall was, I felt a sense of urgency to disclose that to him. It felt wrong for Conall to be in the dark about it. I'd used Mason's need to speak to Calliope as an excuse. I hoped it didn't all backfire and send Conall running.

As long as Dog believed what Linc had disclosed this morning, there shouldn't be an issue with Chosen Few. But I'd heard Dog's reaction, and he hadn't seemed happy.

"Kyle, you gonna ink me or just keep staring at my leg?" Brooklyn asked. A nervous laugh followed as she looked at the half-done tattoo and back to me.

The tribal cuff around her lower leg had roses in the artwork. Inking the flowers was the last part, and what I was supposed to be doing instead of thinking about Conall. How long had I been staring? I gave an apologetic smile. "Was thinking about how amazing this will look when we finish the other leg too."

She beamed at me. "You did a great job of coming up with the concept. I'm stoked with how this one looks." She heaved a heavy sigh, the smile dipping. "I've still got a ways to go before I'll have enough saved for the next one."

Grinning at her, I raised my tattoo gun. "Artwork that is there for life ain't cheap, sweetheart." I got back to inking her leg and attempted to keep my thoughts on what I was doing.

An hour later, I waved goodbye to a thrilled Brooklyn. Her response made the job so worthwhile. It was why I'd been so intrigued with tattooing in the first place. The thrill of getting my first one and seeing the magic of the artwork come alive on the person. Nothing beat it.

I forced myself to clean up my space before checking for any sounds coming from Linc's room. He had several clients booked today. At the sound of his ink gun, I walked off toward the stairs, tugging on the hem of my button-down while going up.

No one was in the kitchen, and the living room door was closed. I hesitated, then knocked. At Mason's shouted, "Come in," I popped my head around the door.

Conall had his back to me, looking out the window. Linc's T-shirt stretched across the width of Conall's very rigid back. He looked as if a strong wind would snap him. He was so tense. Calliope was on the couch. A crumpled pile of tissues sat in her lap, and she had one in her hand. Her eyes were puffy and red-rimmed. Her face was flushed, highlighting the bruising. The atmosphere in the room crackled with tension. The kind that made my stomach dive to the floor.

Mason sat opposite her, dressed casually in jeans and a pale-blue checkered button-down. He held a large legal pad and pen. The page was full, and several dangled toward the floor, showing how much Mason had already written.

"Anyone need a drink, something to eat? I'm stopping for a late lunch." It was the best I could come up with. I hadn't eaten, and all the coffee I'd drank made me jittery. I blamed that when the feeling in the pit of my stomach got worse when Conall didn't bother looking in my direction.

Mason offered me a grateful smile. "Yeah, a break now would be good." He glanced back at Calliope. "Want a Diet Coke? Or are we gonna go for a full sugar hit?"

The smile, though small, moved to her eyes as they crinkled at the edges. "I'll take the full sugar one, please."

"Con?" I asked when he showed no signs of turning around.

It didn't hit me that I'd shortened his name until Mason's brows rose.

"I'll take whatever has caffeine in it." Con's answer came out choked as if he'd struggled to speak past a throat that hurt.

"Mason? What do you want?" I didn't look in Mason's direction. My gaze was still on Conall, who seemed happy to keep facing the window, making the urge to wrap my arms around him a punch to the gut.

"Coke, please, and there are some makings for sandwiches in the refrigerator. Would you mind making up a plate?"

"Can do." I slipped back out, found a tray in the kitchen, and got to work filling it while listening out. A muffled conversation came down the hallway, but it was too hard to figure out who was talking.

Blowing out a breath, I carried the loaded tray into the room five minutes later. Glasses, cans of Coke, and several thick roast beef sandwiches piled on plates. My gaze drifted straight to Conall, who was still in the same spot, as I chatted inanely. "I found some beef, so I used that. Who wants a glass for their Coke?"

"Thanks, Kyle. Just the can for me." Calliope took the Coke I offered her and opened it.

Once she'd had a drink, I lifted a plate, which she took with a nod of thanks. Plate in her lap, I waited to make sure she was okay before I carried a plate over to Conall with a Coke.

It was then I got a look at his face. It was as blotchy as Calliope's. His eyes were puffy and red-rimmed, and my heart broke for him. What Calliope had relayed to Mason had to be hard, and though I didn't have a sister, it didn't take much imagination to figure it had to hurt listening to what her step-daddy had done to her.

With my hands full of the can of Coke and plate, I knocked him with my shoulder in a brotherly manner when he showed no signs of acknowledging my presence. An edge of desperation crept over me when a shudder rippled through him. It was as if he'd transferred some of the pain to me. The strangled noise he made between a sob and a choked cough broke me.

Fuck it!

I glanced about, looking for a place to put down the stuff I held. In the end, I placed it on the floor, then wrapped my arms around his waist, tugging him to me. It was no mean feat with how much bigger he was than me and how unyielding. His eyes did not meet mine.

He didn't move for several tense seconds, then shuddered violently and buried his face into my neck, shivering.

The room disappeared around us as large hands ran over my shoulders and held me close enough there was no room for air between us. Muscles rippled and flexed under his T-shirt as hot breath hit my neck repeatedly.

Wordlessly, I rubbed my hands up and down his back as he continued to shudder. My shower gel and soap clung to his skin as I inhaled shakily, overwhelmed by the need to make this better for him. Hands flexed in the middle of my back. My button-down took the brunt of his feelings when he twisted the material tight enough that I could feel the strain on the buttons.

Muted conversation filtered through, and eventually, when Conall stopped shaking, I acknowledged the other people staring at us.

When had Linc shown up?

Linc's dark eyes held a level of scrutiny I was used to, but that didn't mean I was ready to talk about whatever this was between Conall and me. If it was anything.

"Come and sit down," Linc stated in a tone no one argued with.

Conall finally lifted his head and met my gaze head-on. The conflict crossing his tight features didn't tell me if the show of weakness would bring up more barriers or keep them down.

I hoped it was the latter. One more squeeze, and Conall let go, avoiding eye contact. He bent and picked up the full plate and Coke can, going to where Calliope was sitting, still holding the same sandwich that barely had three bites out of it. Her hair fell about her face, concealing her thoughts.

Shit. Awkward much!

Had she ever witnessed her brother hugging another man?

Mason flipped the legal pad closed and laid it on the table in front of him, diverting my thoughts. He grabbed his glass of Coke and drank deeply. Once empty, he placed it down and reached out to Linc, intertwining their fingers, gazes locking.

At a loss at what I should do, I hesitated before going over and sitting on the other side of Calliope, unsure how Conall would react if I took the seat next to him when he still hadn't looked at me.

Once sitting, I grabbed my abandoned Coke and emptied the can, hoping to get rid of the dryness in my mouth. No longer in the mood for food, I left the plate I'd made for myself untouched. Also, I was unsure I could stomach food because my emotions were riding me harder than the one time I'd ridden Titan in Arlington. The roller coaster kept my stomach feeling out of sorts for days afterward. Conall was sure good at that. However, the sucker-punched look he wore, yeah, I had no defense against that.

The sound of Mason clearing his throat brought my gaze to him from Conall.

"I think I got everything I need. With the picture evidence Liz took and the...swabs...and Calliope's statement of events, there will be plenty for me to work with. Right now, reaching out to the hospital isn't necessary after Dog's visit. He supplied me with all the relevant information concerning Earl's condition. With the cops involved, it will only look suspicious if I seek answers."

Conall stared at Linc. "Did you tell Dog where I was?"

Not what I expected Conall to ask, my nerves jangled as I frowned at Linc. His hair shifted over his shoulders at the nod. "Thought it was best."

"Yeah. The fucking best for who? Did he tell you they'd already judged me and found me guilty?"

Linc came forward in his seat, letting go of Mason's hand. "I explained the situation."

"Yeah, it was too late. They'd already decided I was a thief and guilty of fucking Earl up for money." Conall's voice was devoid of any emotion.

Calliope tucked the hair behind her ear and glanced at her brother. "What are we gonna do?" Her voice was a broken whisper.

"You'll stay with me," I said before I could get my thoughts in order. My heart thundered at her distress.

Mason frowned. "Can we take a step back?" His tone was gentle, but the look he threw at me warned me to keep silent for now. "Are you saying Dog has kicked you out of Chozen Few?" He glanced at Linc with an unspoken question in his eyes.

"I left before they pushed me out. I want no part of a chapter that doesn't have my back. It seems they didn't know me well enough." When he shrugged, it was jerky. "I can't trust them, so I told Dog to keep my patch."

The frown Mason wore deepened. "Is it that easy?" he asked the room in general.

"Can be if the president deems it best for the club." Linc glanced from Mason to Conall. "Was it mutually agreed?"

"He said I know how to get in touch if I change my mind." Conall's lips pursed.

"So you're gonna stay?" I asked before anyone else could speak. The eagerness I couldn't hide got a glower from Linc and had Mason's lips twitching.

Conall twisted his head in my direction. He held my gaze, and I struggled to figure out what thoughts were running through his head.

Mind reading right then would have been a big plus.

The tension in the room increased with the silence, then Conall looked away toward Linc. "Would it be a problem if we stayed?"

Say no! Say no! Say no!

My hand gripped the empty Coke can as I waited for Linc to answer.

Linc's headshake was slow, followed by a thoughtful look that helped unknot my stomach. "If you're planning on staying, you'll need a job. Mason will need to look at legal guardianship. Calliope will need to transfer schools, so they'll need to transfer her transcripts. You'll also need to get your belongings from Round Rock." Linc glanced at me. "You got any plans for tomorrow?"

"No, why?" I had a good idea what he was after, but I didn't jump the gun.

"You're going on a road trip."

Mason laid a hand on Linc's arm. "The cops will be monitoring the trailer for sure. Or someone will be. Taking things from a crime scene is illegal."

"I trust you to make sure it's not an issue, and when we're going, no one but the rats will be interested," Linc answered with a smile that caused Mason to shiver and his eyes to darken with what looked like desire.

I glanced away, not wanting to see the pair getting hot for each other. My gaze collided with Conall's, and I smiled reassuringly. "You up for a road trip with me?"

Chapter Eleven

Conall

As Kyle drove the truck, the headlights highlighted the empty road. The radio played Ray LaMontagne, and Kyle hummed along. The soulful lyrics seemed to have meaning as the man crooned about making it through. But I wasn't so sure if I'd cut off my nose to spite my face after having all afternoon and evening to stew in my own juices. Mason had asked more questions about Calliope's guardianship, and I hadn't been able to answer if my mom had actually appointed Earl. Embarrassed at not knowing, I'd been glad Kyle had returned to work. I had no clue where Mom's paperwork was. Mason had tasked me with finding it so he could see what my mom's wishes had been and what he'd need to do to get Earl out of our lives.

After Mom's death, I'd been gutted and hadn't thought to check. I could see now that I'd been foolish. Mom had nothing except the trailer, and that was a shit pit. Earl had moved in with them. Then they'd gotten married shortly after, so I'd assumed everything was his after she died. He'd often said he could make us homeless, and I hadn't questioned whether it was true. I stayed for one reason: Calliope.

If I was honest, Mason's questions rattled me. What if we'd been putting up with Earl for no good reason? Had my apathy put Calliope in harm's way?

My heaved sigh got Kyle's gaze swinging toward me before returning to the road. "You can change the music if you want. We're not that far now. You'll need to guide me where to go when we hit Round Rock."

"Why do you wanna help me?" I blurted out, suddenly wanting an answer before Kyle saw where I'd lived, which was nothing like his home.

The truck slowed as Kyle glanced back in my direction. His shoulders moved up, and a few seconds passed. In the shadowy cab interior, it was hard to make out what Kyle was thinking as his brows drew together. The silence between us stretched, and I thought he wouldn't answer when he finally spoke, "Are we gonna pretend there ain't any chemistry between us?"

I liked his straightforward approach. It was refreshing and attractive, but the dip in my stomach signaled my disappointment over that being the only reason. "Are you saying that's why you offered to let us stay? So you could fuck me?"

Breath hissed past his teeth before he cursed, and then the truck swerved onto the side of the road, coming to a harsh stop. The seatbelt tightened hard against my chest, then relaxed.

Kyle shifted in his seat, the engine ticking as he glared at me. "I'm not gonna deny that the idea of fucking isn't appealing. I'd be lying if I did after the kiss we shared. Heck, even before that. I want to get to know you and your sister. I wanna help you both. You deserve a break. I hate this whole situation."

Kyle ran shaking hands through his hair, messing it up, tugging on the attraction simmering between us. "When Linc's sister died giving birth to River, I was there for him. Another fucked-up situation I offered to help with 'cause Mom raised me to help offers when they need it. I've been told I'm a bleeding heart, and maybe I am, but I have space in my apartment, and you need it. And when you've got things figured out, you can pay me back if you feel the need. Not that I care about that, so we're clear."

A passing car lit up the cab's interior, highlighting Kyle's glittering eyes. He scrubbed a hand over them. "It hurts my damn heart when I think about what that fucker did to your sister. So, no, it's not just about wanting to get in your pants." As if trying to lighten the mood, he winked salaciously at me. "Though if the offer is there, I'd be more than happy to take you up on it."

I had whiplash from all the twists and turns of the conversation and what I recalled from the first night I'd seen him. It appeared I wasn't ready to let the topic drop when I pointed to the preppy outfit. "I don't think I'm what you're looking for." I lifted my chin. "That night at Shorty's, you were working hard to get the attention of the snooty prick who looked like his button-down was choking the life out of him. Back then, you dressed far more casually. Now you wear that get-up. I ain't never gonna date someone who ain't happy with who he is and feels the need to change to meet some other fucker's perception of what they want." I was bummed to say it aloud, but stringing a guy along was never my thing, regardless of how hot he was or the epic level of attraction.

"That told me," Kyle muttered, sounding pissed.

I wasn't sure whether it was at me, him, or both of us as he twisted back in his seat and pulled back onto the highway.

The music was the only sound in the cab as Kyle's hands gripped the steering wheel, his gaze firmly fixed on the road, his posture stiff.

The cussing I did was all in my head. This was why I'd kept out of Kyle's way when we'd returned to his apartment. It mentally fucked me listening to Calliope relive what Earl did. It was one of the hardest things I'd experienced in my life. The beating I'd taken from four members of a rival club when I'd been alone the year before was nothing. I'd take that hands-down over the images Calliope had painted in my head. The horror of what she'd endured would forever live in my heart. Being vulnerable in front of Kyle had crept up on me, and when he'd hugged me, I'd nearly broken down.

My inability to support Calliope financially, mentally, and physically was bad enough right now that I couldn't stomach Kyle's pity. I'd ruthlessly shoved aside the pity party because Calliope didn't deserve that from me. She needed me to man up. And if that meant eating my pride and being honest with Kyle, I would, but not when I'd just had my heart ripped out of my chest by the claws of Calliope's terror.

I had mixed feelings about staying at Kyle's place because of his damn bleeding heart. Yeah, I was the one who'd taken dating off the fucking table, but that didn't mean I wasn't a contradictory asshole. This was why I didn't date. It was too fucking complicated.

You aren't dating, a snarky voice pointed out.

It was easier to think about Linc and work. But that wasn't much better when I recalled Dog had mentioned Linc had gone legit, and I had no actual skills worth a damn. I was a great lookout and had a solid back for heavy lifting. I could fight hard when the need arose, only none of that would work for Linc. Would it?

Mom hammered independence into me early on. I'd earned my way since the age of nine, running errands, not asking questions. When I'd approached Chosen Few to become a prospect, they'd already known who I was because I'd done plenty of errands for them. I was good at keeping my mouth shut and my head down. I didn't poke my nose in business that wasn't mine. I had hardly any schooling, so how the fuck was I gonna find a job to pay our way? Linc hadn't said much more on the subject after the topic went to Calliope staying the night at their place, sleeping in River's bed.

I'd gotten the feeling it wouldn't be the last time we'd talk about work. I'd need to figure out what, if anything, I could suggest doing to earn my way. He didn't seem like a man who didn't keep his word.

Would he take on a new prospect?

I tapped my knee in time to the music. Was that the answer? If he was legit, then how would that work?

The truck slowed again, and my gaze traveled to the road sign. Fuck, time was up. We were here.

"You're gonna need to direct me to your trailer park."

The low timbre of his voice tugged something deep in my belly. Ignoring it, I considered the safest route to get where we needed to be. "Take the next right, then follow the road until you come to a crossroads, then go left. There's a road that leads into the park that ain't used that often." In the truck's dimness, I caught the eyebrow raise. "It's more like a dirt road track. Lots of potholes, so you'll need to take it slow. I'm sure Killer doesn't want you wrecking his truck."

Kyle nodded and followed my directions. When the lights hit the road we needed to take, Kyle hissed out a breath. "You weren't fucking kidding. That ain't a dirt track. Fuck, it's got craters."

Kyle's jaw bunched as he slowed to a snail's pace and crawled down the road. The truck bounced and rocked, and I held onto the oh-shit bar after my ass left the seat for the third time, and I nearly cracked my head on the top of the cab.

I hadn't worried about Linc's truck being big enough to hold everything we owned because it wasn't much. However, I hadn't considered whether it would make it to the trailer park in one piece. Especially with the high probability we could be wasting time since my brothers might have trashed my stuff. They weren't a forgiving bunch when they thought a brother had betrayed them. The road was much worse than I remembered. Or it could be that it was much easier to skip past the enormous holes on a motorcycle.

"Shit," Kyle said for the third time in a thready voice, as his teeth seemed to rattle together. "How much farther?"

"Not far. See there." I pointed to the dim lights of the homes in the distance. "You might wanna pull up at the next bend so you can do a U-turn."

"Fuck that. I'll risk going back on the main road. I'm not sure the truck can handle much more. And I certainly don't think Linc would appreciate his suspension being left behind on this shitty excuse for a road!"

I chuckled at how he warbled like a bird as he bounced along. It was that or curse along with him, and he was doing plenty of that for both of us.

He scowled, or I thought he did, when he quickly glanced in my direction before looking back at the road. "It fucking ain't funny, and I'm gonna make you pay for this! I don't think my teeth or ass will ever be the same again."

At the bend where I'd told him to pull over, he continued on. There was no point sighing. I didn't blame him. My teeth were getting the same treatment. "When you reach the entrance to the trailer park, turn left and go straight ahead." I kept directing him, making him pull up behind my old trailer, lights switched off so as not to draw any attention. The moon and a few lights helped guide us and show exactly what a dump the place was.

Engine off, I got out of the truck, working to keep my thoughts on what Kyle would make of it all at the back of my mind. I reached into the back of the truck for the bags Kyle had loaned me. The stench of garbage was heavy in the air. A male voice followed the sound of a dog barking in the distance, cussing up a storm.

When Kyle got out of the truck, carefully shutting the door, I wordlessly pointed to the side of the trailer. He followed closely. He treaded as carefully as me as we rounded the side, heading to the steps. I glanced cautiously at the other trailers close enough to see us. Lights were off, and no one seemed to stir. It was three a.m. I'd picked this time, knowing it was the quietest time of the night.

I avoided the squeaky third step, showing Kyle where to step. Key in the lock, the door opened soundlessly, and I quickly stepped into the dark trailer. Stale air, urine, the coppery undertones of blood and sweat lingered in the stuffy place, turning my stomach.

Avoiding looking at Kyle, I dropped the bags to pull out my phone to put the flashlight on, keeping it low to the ground. The shadowy light didn't disguise what a shit hole the place was. Cracked furniture, peeling paint, and general neglect. The place looked pretty much as it had when I'd left, minus the body on the floor. Blood stains remained, though someone had picked up the broken TV.

Kyle brushed against my arm and leaned in. "Where do you want me to start?"

I glanced about, wondering where Mom had kept her personal papers and where Earl had kept his. And what else we needed. Calliope wanted her things, so I sent him into her room, uncertain what might have become of my stuff. Kyle didn't need to see my shame.

Once he'd disappeared into Calliope's bedroom with two bags, I went to the side cabinet next to the TV and rooted through the drawers. Working one-handed was hard as I crouched to keep hidden and kept the flashlight closer to the ground, squinting at the writing on the letters in the drawers.

I gave up when I heard Kyle heading back to me. Realizing I'd wasted a lot of time, I shoved everything into the smallest bag I had.

He bent next to me, his hot breath touching my ear as he whispered, "I've got everything out of the drawers. Is there anything else you need me to grab?"

I shook my head. "Take this bag and what you've got, and wait in the truck. I'll pack my shit now," I answered, keeping my voice low.

His response was to take the bag from my outstretched hand and head to the door. He disappeared into the night, and I grabbed the other two bags and went to my room.

I braced as I nudged the door open fully with my foot. In the casting light, everything appeared undisturbed as far as I could make out. If the cops had been through my stuff, they hadn't messed anything up.

My hidey-hole wasn't in the trailer, so I had no fear they'd find anything important here. I'd never trusted Earl. What I wanted no one to find was outside, around the back, under the trailer where I stored the junk. I'd kept a small tin box for things that were valuable to me.

My pulse leaped at every creaking noise as I stuffed clothes into the bags. As I went through the trailer that I never thought I'd come back to, the feelings the place gave me ensured I'd never return. It was no longer home, now tainted by Earl's violation of my sister. It could burn to the ground for all I cared.

Out the door with the bulging bags, I locked the door.

"Who's out there?" Old Man Wilkin's called.

Fuck.

I debated before I swung around to see the old coot coming out his front door, a cigarette hanging from his lips. Emaciated and looking like a strong wind would snap him in two, his lips pulled into a sneer. The cigarette hung from his lower lip before he moved it to the corner of his mouth. The baggy off-white T-shirt had several burn holes, as did the lounge pants, which were neither black nor gray, an in-between color. Diagnosed with cancer a year ago, he remained defiant and smoked his sixty cigarettes daily. I should have expected he'd be up.

He hated me for reasons I could never fathom.

"You robbin' the place while Earl is laid up in the hospital? Didn't expect nothin' less from the likes of you." He sniffed and sat on the stool he used to have a smoke.

"Ain't taken anything but what belongs to me. The fucker is welcome to the rest. You just mind your business and keep your mouth shut, or else!" I growled, giving him a hard stare before turning on my heel to walk away. He was as toxic as everyone else in this place, and with no need to linger, I released my first real breath of relief since I'd found Calliope.

A hacking coughing fit followed a snort as I slipped around the trailer. After glancing to check that no one was watching, I dropped my bags to dig under the pile of junk. My heart rate settled when I felt the tin box. The weight suggested it had been untouched. I dusted off the dirt and lifted the lid. My pulse settling, I shut it and shoved it into the top of the nearest bag.

Time to get the hell out of dodge.

Chapter Twelve

Kyle

Tired and feeling out of sorts after the late night and conversation with Conall on the drive to Round Rock, I rolled over and dragged the pillow over my face, giving up on trying to sleep. The sun had risen hours ago, filtering through the blinds, and the hunger in the pit of my stomach suggested I should feed it. Too exhausted to do more than acknowledge it, I groaned mournfully into my pillow.

The image of Conall's grim expression when we'd parked at the back of the trailer had changed to something cold and hard when we'd entered his home. My heart ached at what he was possibly reliving. He'd barely looked at me when he'd requested I pack Calliope's things. I'd checked out the other rooms as I'd passed, and I realized pretty fast why Conall struggled to accept anything at face value. I was a giver. I'd been taught to share. Mom had been sure to explain not everyone was as lucky as us. Conall's home suggested he'd had little growing up, not that material things counted, but I suspected love had been in short supply too.

It made the drive back to Belton even more difficult, and not just because of what had happened before we arrived. There was something about Conall that tugged at all the feels inside me. I'd been "in love" and had hookups. I knew the difference between real and casual. When Conall talked about dating, I sensed he meant casual, or maybe it was what I hoped.

When we'd returned, and with how tense the silence was between us, I'd left Conall in the living room with the excuse of needing sleep. Had I slept? Fuck no. I'd spent more time tossing and turning, going over the whole "I'm not gonna date you" talk.

He was right. I had tried to change myself to meet someone else's expectations. It was a little lowering to realize I'd felt so desperate for a date that I'd lost sight of myself. I didn't blame Conall for not wanting to date someone who acted like that, like me. That didn't mean it didn't fucking hurt.

Unconsciously, I rubbed at the center of my chest before dragging the pillow off my face at the sound of heavy foot tread in the hallway. I lifted my head off the mattress and strained to hear. Was Conall hovering outside the door?

I'd thought long and hard about how to change his perception, to get him to see that wasn't who I really was.

The tap on wood had me shooting up and placing the pillow behind me as I shouted, "Yeah?" then lounged back on the bed, aiming for sexily rumpled as I pushed the cover down a little to reveal more naked chest. There was no harm in that. No one could see me making a fool of myself.

Except Conall! The snippy voice was back.

Hadn't he been real specific when he told me he wasn't interested in losers?

Before I could yank the cover back up, the door creaked open to reveal a dressed Conall.

My panicked throughs fled as my gaze traveled down the man who looked all kinds of hot and sexy. Freshly showered, judging by the dampness of his hair brushed back off his gorgeous face, he smelled of my body wash. The T-shirt hugged his broad chest like a second skin.

Shit, that was the one he'd worn the night I'd first seen him. Had he done that on purpose? The jeans hugged his thick legs. I gulped at the faded denim around his upper thighs that highlighted exactly what he had to offer. He lounged against the doorframe, his arms crossed over his chest, making them bulge, and I forgot how to breathe with memories of the first time we'd eye-fucked.

What was he playing at?

When he didn't seem inclined to talk... his gaze lingering on my tattooed chest, I exhaled gustily. "Whassup?" Sounding breathless was not what I'd hoped for, which kept me from checking Conall's reaction.

"Was gonna head out to get some breakfast. Wanna join me? A thank you for helpin' me."

My head jerked to meet his gaze, and I caught the shoulder shrug like it was nothing. His tone gave zero away, though part of me was convinced there was interest in his eyes when they drifted back to my naked chest.

My nipples pebbled under the sheer concentration of the stare. It was hard to remain still with the urge to move my legs to hide my growing reaction. The intensity was like a physical stroke to my dick.

"Well?" One brow arched, and heat flooded my cheeks at having not answered.

"Yeah, that would be good. Just give me ten to shower and dress."

He nodded, and I expected him to move, but he didn't. He continued to lounge on the doorframe as if waiting for me to get out of bed.

What kind of mind game was this? Last night, he'd clearly said he wasn't interested. Yes, the kiss we'd shared had been off-the-charts hot. Was this my chance to show him I was genuinely interested and prepared to act like me? Then a thought struck.

Did he realize I was naked under the covers?

The hesitation lasted two more seconds.

Fuck it. I liked to flirt, and though I didn't have a gym body, I could hold my own. I had good legs, solid thighs, a great ass, and though I was a little round around the middle, I had a nice seven-inch cock I was proud of. Always shaven in case of some impromptu situation... like now, I had nothing to lose, and if he wanted a show, I could give him that!

Inhaling, I held his gaze as I pushed the covers off my legs and got out of bed. There was the smallest of noises, like a gasp, but his gaze revealed zilch.

Semi-hard, my cock thickened at his slow perusal of my body like a hot caress. I stood and waited for his gaze to return to mine. The flush of desire riding his cheekbones, shrunken pupils, and flared nostrils gave him away.

Encouraged, I didn't think about the previous rejection. Hips rolling sexily, or so I hoped, I walked toward Conall. Stopping close enough to feel the heat of his body, I didn't miss how his biceps expanded, as if he was working on holding himself still.

Offering a cocky smile, I leaned close enough that my naked chest brushed his folded arms. My nipples tingled at the feel of hair teasing them. My cock pulsed, and the sexual tension caused my skin to buzz. It was real. There was no mistaking the bulge in his jeans as I glanced down between us. "Like what you see?"

He wet his lips, head nodding slowly, and the need to taste him drove me forward. I was versatile, but I loved to be pinned and fucked hard. Right now, I wanted to prove that Conall was wrong about me, even if he'd been right about his observations. As our mouths touched, his arms unfolded, and he dragged me to him. The taste of mint lingered on his breath as his lips parted and the kiss became hungry. My dick pressed up against Conall's clothed cock. The barrier did little to tame the wild storm brewing inside me. The frustration of the last twenty-four hours disappeared as we ground against each other. Uncaring I was smearing pre-cum over his jeans, I gasped when his hands stroked down my body and around to grip my ass hard enough to bruise.

Swung around, my back hit the chilly wall. "Humph," I grunted into Conall's mouth, not stopping as he caged me in and rolled his hips in a slow, sexy grind that didn't match the hunger of the lips devouring mine. Shivers from the coldness of the wall and what Conall was doing competed as goose-bumps rose over my arms and legs.

He bit my bottom lip hard enough to send a spark of desire right to my cock, which I rubbed against his, needing more. Fingers curled and unfurled repeatedly on my ass. I hooked my thigh around his hip, pushing into each roll and grind against me.

I panted when he kissed his way over my jaw to my ear and down my neck. His teeth raked over the sensitive skin, making it burn. My hands tugged at the hem of his T-shirt, desperate to feel his skin against mine. I pushed it up hastily, dragging it over his head, stopping him briefly in his exploration. His tongue got frisky with my left nipple. He sucked the hard bud between his lips and clasped his teeth around it, increasing the pressure until I thought I'd go crazy.

I was a nipple slut, and my cock throbbed as if something directly connected the two while lips, tongue, and teeth drove me crazy. Conall hit all my hotspots when a finger slipped between my butt cheeks and rubbed at the puckered flesh in slow circles. It was impossible to figure out what to focus on with how my body vibrated like his own personal tuning fork, seeking what Conall could give me.

The finger from my ass disappeared, and I was about to complain when his hand came up to my lips. His teeth bit hard enough to get a long, drawn-out moan and a finger dipping between my parted lips. Instinctively, I sucked, and Conall made a guttural sound at the back of his throat that vibrated through my nipple, sending fresh waves of desire to my cock. I slid my tongue up the length of the thick digit like it was his dick, getting more sounds and sensations that edged me closer to the point of no return.

Were we really doing this?

When Conall's mouth released my spit-coated nipple and the air hit it, the throb of my cock increased, answering my question.

I blinked owlishly at Conall, trying to get my head to register what his lips were saying.

"Come on, Ky, get it nice and wet so I can feel what it's like to sink into your tight ass," he growled huskily as he wiggled his finger in my mouth. Needing no more encouragement than that visual, I salivated all over it.

Conall pulled his finger out of my mouth, and a string of saliva dripped down my chin before it disappeared back between my ass cheeks. I lifted my leg higher on his hip, opening myself more to him. I mewled in pleasure as he kissed my wet chin and licked up my spit before kissing me hard and punishingly as the wet finger pushed into my ass, stealing my ability to think about how he'd changed the pace from slow to fast.

"Oh, motherfucker," I hissed, drawing back, gasping for air.

But he followed. The kiss blistered my skin with its heat. His aim in my ass was good and brushed directly over my hot spot. The force of the initial intrusion bled to pleasure before my brain could fully register the pain. He swallowed every sound I made as his mouth and finger made it impossible to stop and take stock of what was about to happen.

My cock trapped between our bodies throbbed, my ball sac tightened, and my eyes clenched, as did my ass as cum splattered all over Conall's jeans and my stomach. His hips ground against mine, and the cock beneath the material bucked. Conall made a sound in the back of his throat as if in pain as his hips stuttered.

I ran my hands absently up his sweat-coated back as Conall finally released my mouth to lay his sticky forehead on my shoulder. Hot breaths ran down my damp chest, making my sensitive nipples pebble. Conall sucked in deep, greedy gulps of air, his body shaking against mine.

Eyes shut, my head thumped against the wall as I held on to Conall, limp and satisfied in a way I hadn't been in a very long time. The finger slipped from my ass, and I felt the loss as Conall pulled back. The weight of his stare on me made me see there was no way to avoid what came next. Would he regret what we'd done? Fuck, I hoped not.

When his finger traced over my cheekbone, my eyelids flickered open. I searched his expression, looking for regret. What I saw was a lazy look of pure satisfaction and... something I couldn't name. It didn't seem negative. Maybe it was my sex-hazed glasses?

"You okay?" he finally rasped in a deep husky voice I could listen to all day.

Was I? "Yeah, fuck, I just emptied my balls in the most spectacular fashion all over you. I suppose I should feel bad about messin' you up, but I'm too blissed out right now to care. So what's not to be okay about?" My stomach snarled loudly, and my lips moved into a lazy grin. "Did someone mention treating me to breakfast?"

Chapter Thirteen

Conall

Brain coming back online, the sticky mess in my underwear and over my jeans ensured I didn't miss that I'd lost my fucking mind. I shut the bedroom door behind me and leaned against it. Shutting my eyes didn't help when it heightened my sense of smell. Sex and Kyle's scent clung to me. I groaned.

It was a fucking epic mess. One I'd created all because a sexily rumpled man had... what? What had he done? Accepted my invitation to breakfast, nothing more. What was I playing at? Why hadn't I just left the room?

I thumped my head against the door in disgust at the reality that I'd gone in, perversely wanting to provoke him. When he'd left me not that many hours ago looking like I'd kicked his puppy, I hadn't been able to get him out of my head. Maybe it was cutting the last ties to Round Rock by taking my things and understanding that I would never return. Unless the cops hauled my ass back, and that was still a possibility.

Opening my eyes, I flicked a glance around the room Kyle had generously offered. Pale lemon-colored walls, thick carpet on the floor, a bed big enough for me to stretch out on. It was simple, yet so much more than what I'd had my whole life. I was a simple man. I didn't need much. A roof over my head and a full belly, friends I could call family, and Calliope safe. I'd blown the last two and taken away the roof over my head by acting without thinking.

Now I'd lost my mind. Or why else would I have provoked the situation in Kyle's bedroom? I wanted to kick my ass. I hated guys who gave off mixed signals, and that was exactly what I'd done. First, I'm telling him I'm not interested, then I'm fucking humping him against the goddamn wall like some sex-starved animal driven by pure instinct to mate. Honesty led me to groan at the reason. Insecurity. I'd wanted to prove that after seeing the shit hole I'd come from that Kyle didn't see me differently, regardless of what I'd said to him in the truck. It was fucking pathetic.

Life felt like it was giving me a curveball, but I'd gone in the direction of a screwball. Royally trying to screw my ass with my stupidity. I rubbed my eyes, trying to remove the image of Kyle looking good enough to eat with all those damn hot tattoos on his chest. Tattooed guys had always been my weakness. The artwork on his arm and the one side of his chest was clearly Linc's, but there were other tattoos lower on his abdomen that I suspected could be Kyle's work. I'd taken the time to look at his artwork and style of tattooing. Shoot me, I was bored, and the artwork hung right there on the walls. What else was I supposed to do when boredom kicked in?

I dragged myself away from the door. The tattoos were easier to think about than what just happened and why. Kyle's style was as distinct as Linc's. The guy had talent with a gun, for sure.

In the small bathroom attached to the bedroom, I shucked off my jeans and underwear, the drying cum evidence of my madness. I huffed a loud sigh as I wet a cloth and cleaned myself. Dried, I headed back to find clean clothes.

There was a sound in the hallway, and I realized I'd been procrastinating too long. I quickly rooted through the bag I hadn't bothered to unpack and now didn't see the point because Kyle might change his mind since I was messing with his head.

I pulled out fresh jeans. I slipped them on and zipped them up, not bothering with underwear.

I cursed over where my head was when I noticed the lack of a T-shirt and where I'd left it. "Shit!" I pulled a clean one from the bag and slipped it on.

The noises I could hear indicated Kyle was ready. Seeing no way to go back out now without looking like an asshole, I headed out the door after retrieving my wallet from my dirty jeans.

I came to a standstill at the sight of Kyle in the kitchen area drinking from a Coke can. He was dressed much as he had been the first time I'd seen him. The preppy clothes were nowhere in sight. Soft denim hugged his thighs, showing off the lean legs I'd seen naked. The Wild River band T-shirt was loose, and he'd tucked the front part into his jeans, revealing a retro Harley Davidson belt buckle. Fuck, that was hot!

He pulled the can from his lips and offered it over. "Want some? I needed a caffeine boost." The flirty smile was lethal with the way he was now dressed. He ticked all my hot buttons, and I was sure steam was coming from the collar of my T-shirt with the memory of what we'd done there between us. The air crackled with the sexual tension that had been present since our very first encounter.

This is such a bad idea!

But it seemed I was the king of bad ideas as I walked to him and took the can, placing my lips where his had been and drinking deeply. The caffeine boosted my system, but not as much as the eyes gazing at me when I licked the rim of the can, catching a drop before giving it back to him.

"I can think of better things to lick," he teased before he sucked the rim.

In the pit of my stomach, desire swirled fast and tightened in my groin. It was far too easy to imagine him doing that to any part of me.

I sucked in a breath. His fresh scent wouldn't let me get my bearings as I glanced away and back.

"I thought you were hungry?" It was the first thing my stupid brain could come up with when I floundered from the impulse to pick him up, throw him over the counter, and fuck him until he couldn't remember his own name.

When I hadn't moved earlier in the bedroom, I'd been the one to issue the invitation. This time, it was there in Kyle's penetrating stare. It was as if he was looking deep inside me, and regardless of the nasty shit I'd done and the crappy place I'd lived, he was still interested.

But no one stuck around long for me. I knew this, and confusion warred with desire until Kyle placed the can down and took hold of my hand as if sensing my battle. The lazy grin I liked appeared as he tugged me toward the door. "I am. Where did you want to go for breakfast?" He glanced at me, upping the cheekiness of the smile. "Seein' as you're payin'."

Did he think this was a date?

Wasn't it? You asked him out for food! Back was the snarky voice that I hated.

I shook off the unease climbing up my spine. I'd Googled the area to check out where was good to eat on the off chance I'd venture out when being stuck inside got too much. "Miller's Smokehouse on Central Avenue looks good. Unless you have somewhere else you wanna go?"

"Nah, Miller's is good. They do great pancake platters. And I'm starvin'." He beamed and winked at me before continuing out of the apartment. He didn't release my hand as he closed the door, then headed for the stairs.

Out of the building a minute later, I stared at our joined hands. The warmth and firm clasp were a constant reminder of who I was with. Calliope was the only person I'd ever held hands with, and that had stopped when she could cross the road without me worrying she'd do something impulsive. The unease resurfaced. I had no memory of ever wanting to hold a guy's hand in public. Yes, I'd dated, but nothing too serious, and never would I have thought to take a guy's hand and hold it. That was too... sappy. Wasn't it?

Kyle didn't seem to think so as he headed off in what I assumed was the direction of where we were going. "I've been to Miller's a few times. If you want a recommendation, just ask."

I scratched at my bristly jaw, trying to figure out what the hell was going on. The walk across town was about twenty minutes, and Kyle kept up the constant chatter, occasionally stopping to wave or shout hello to someone on the other side of the street. Each time, I struggled not to pull away from the prying eyes and curiosity. I'd never been one to put myself in the spotlight, and I could feel it now. The sky was blue and cloudless, the sun warm, making it a pleasant day. One to be enjoyed, yet I couldn't think past the hand holding mine.

"Maybe we should go get Calliope," I muttered after the last person came over to inspect me. Clearly, folks liked Kyle, judging by the friendly way they spoke to him.

He stopped, brow pinching. "Shit, I never thought to ask what time you told Linc we'd be around to pick her up."

I didn't miss the "we." Did one kiss and a frot equal a "we?"

God, now it was my turn to be confused because a part of me wanted the "we" more than I'd first thought.

You gave him the big speech only last night! The snippy voice could go take a fucking leap off a tall building.

Kyle tipped his head and stared at me in a way that suggested I'd waited far too long to respond. "Erm, he said to come by when I was ready."

The smile was back. "Cool. Mason will make sure Calliope gets fed, and if not, River will. That girl is a human trash can. She can eat her way through the contents of the kitchen without stopping for a break." He chuckled and continued pulling me along by the hand.

"I remember," I muttered, blushing like I was some innocent virgin on their first date.

"Oh yeah, I forgot for a moment you came to watch over River when we all headed to Washington."

Latching on to that like a man clutching their last straw, I asked, "Did the situation get resolved without bloodshed?"

Linc hadn't said much when he'd returned. He hadn't appeared to have any injuries that suggested there'd been a fight. But they'd come back earlier than I'd expected. It wasn't my business, so I'd kept my mouth shut and my questions to myself. It was what I was good at, only right now, I needed something to talk about that stopped me from thinking about the hand I hadn't shaken off. Each passing minute made me more conscious of it when Kyle occasionally squeezed my fingers.

"It didn't quite go as expected. It disappointed some of my brothers that things didn't get to the 'banging some heads together' stage after Toad's dick of a father had him kidnapped right out front of the clubhouse."

Holy fuck, I hadn't known that. "You shitting me?"

Kyle scowled. "Nope, I wish I was. The fucker sent these two goon assholes with drugs to grab him." He waved his free hand in the air. "Anyway, they didn't get enough of whatever it was into Toad, and when they stopped at a gas station owned by one member of Dark Angels, Toad subdued the guy still in the car and escaped."

He chuckled. "Well, sort of. He tripped and bashed his head and concussed his ass. Sid went nutzo. He's into Toad in a big way. Anyway, we found Toad before things went too far south and got him to the hospital. Mason, who prefers to play by the law, did some whizz lawyerly shit and pinned Toad's father to the wall by his short and curlies. Job done. Toad even inherited a shit ton of money the father intended to keep for himself."

We stopped at a door with a sign above that read Miller's Smokehouse. The scents coming through the door Kyle opened with his free hand made my mouth water as much as the wide and fucking sexy smirk aimed at me. "He gave everyone a gift, which was very cool."

That was a cool thing to do. "Nice," I said as I went ahead of Kyle, who didn't seem inclined to let go of my hand soon.

A waitress wearing a pink T-shirt with the place's logo gave us a welcoming smile after her gaze landed on our joined hands.

"We'll take a table for two if you have one," Kyle said before the girl could speak.

"We most certainly do. Y'all follow me now." She grabbed two menus and weaved her way through the packed place. I kept my gaze high, not looking at anyone.

"Well, look who the cat dragged in," a rough male voice said when we reached the seats by the window. The bald guy had an enormous serpent tattooed on his neck.

I nodded at Serpent, Linc's second in command. I'd met him once at Linc's place. I suspected the man sitting next to him had to be Toad, who Kyle had just been talking about, due to the way they sat pressed together with no gap between them.

"Sid, Toad." Kyle nodded at both men. "Looks like you had the same idea as us."

"Looks like." Serpent's gaze narrowed. "Why don't you join us? We just ordered."

The smile Kyle wore was no longer as big as it had been. Was there an issue with Kyle being seen with me? I discarded that thought, given how the guy had held my hand all the way here. Then what was the problem?

The waitress realized we'd stopped and returned to us, her smile never wavering as she looked between us.

"We're gonna join our friends," Kyle said, finally letting go of my hand to slide into the booth across from the two men eyeing me with lots of interest.

My hand cooled, and I clenched it, uncertain how to feel about the sudden feeling of loss. I slid into the seat, took the menu from the waitress, and pretended interest as she listed off the day's specials. My appetite had deserted me for some reason I didn't want to poke at.

"So, who's your friend?" Toad asked in a friendly tone that did not match Serpent's expression after the waitress left with their order.

Oh, this was gonna be fun! Breakfast and an interrogation.

Chapter Fourteen

Kyle

I didn't need a rocket scientist to figure out why Conall had tensed and nearly broke my fingers when Sid had spoken. I'd worked hard to keep things casual and act like I usually did with a guy who offered to take me out for food. I didn't think too hard about the mixed messages Conall was giving off. I would do my absolute best to be myself at all times around Conall from now on, even in front of my brothers.

"This is Conall. He came and looked after River while we all went to Washington. He's staying at my place right now."

Toad nodded and blushed. "Belton's a good place."

Sid slung his arm over the back of the seat and affectionately squeezed Toad's shoulder in a way that continued to shock the fuck right out of me. The guy had been as closed off as anyone could get about their sexuality until things had gone south with Toad. Then he'd openly declared they were a couple when most of the brothers, including me, hadn't even known Sid was gay.

"So what brings you to Belton, Runner?" The suspicion wasn't disguised as Sid eyed the other man closely. Conall might be a member of a motorcycle chapter we were on friendly terms with, but that did not mean Sid would let his guard down. It was why he made a hell of a second in command. Toad, whose eyes were darting between us, landed on me, and he gave me an odd look I couldn't interpret.

I liked Toad. He had his own shitty past to contend with. Mostly, he'd remained hidden until Sid had, I'd overheard, pushed Toad to stop running. The two couldn't be happier, or that's how it appeared.

After a long pause, and when I was considering I might need to answer, Conall responded, "Family shit. Came to see if Killer...Linc could help me with some things."

Sid's eyebrows arched as he looked me dead in the eyes. "Why is this the first I'm hearing this?"

Shrugging one shoulder, I considered how to respond without pissing off Sid, which was never good. "Linc was away when Con arrived...and things were tricky with Calliope."

"Tricky, how?"

"A member of Chosen Few attacked her, so I retaliated," Conall said, his voice full of challenge. His stare meeting Sid's.

"Linc knows all this?" he asked quietly. The hard edge was unmistakable.

"Yeah, he knows, and so does his boyfriend." Conall was as stiff as a board when Sid cursed at his confession.

"Then maybe after breakfast, we should go back to Linc's so someone can fill me the fuck in too!"

The waitress came with our food, stopping the conversation. Once she'd gone, I steered the conversation away from Conall. "Did you hear that Cammy's picture arrived from Scotland on Friday? Fuck, the guy was bouncing all over the place when he popped by the shop. I only got to see a photo he'd snapped of it. But it was so lifelike, I'd have sworn it was a photo of the dog. She's some artist, that Angela Davidson, with wicked skills to capture the cheekiness of Cammy's beagle." Toad was the one to pay for the Scottish artist to do an original piece of artwork. I wasn't sure how much it cost, but the finished product was as good as any of Linc's tattoos.

Back to blushing, Toad nodded as he chewed the bacon he'd popped into his mouth.

I babbled on until the back of my neck was so tight I was glad I wasn't working until Tuesday. An hour later, we all strolled out onto the street. Sid nodded toward the auto shop truck parked on the other side of the street, and I wondered why I hadn't noticed it. "Want a lift?"

Seeing no other option since we'd walked, and Sid could clearly see there weren't any motorcycles parked, I agreed. "Could you drop me back at my place? I need to return Linc's truck. We borrowed it yesterday."

That got another scowl, and Sid stomped off down the street. Toad shrugged and followed at a slower pace to match mine and Conall's. We got in the back seat, and I braced, knowing Sid as I did. The man could get real vocal if he thought folks were holding out on him.

We'd barely got comfortable when Sid twisted in the seat and demanded angrily. "Why did you need the truck? What the fuck am I missing?"

I sighed and rubbed my forehead. "A lot, but it's complicated." I glanced at Conall, giving him an encouraging smile. "Maybe you should explain before Sid loses his shit."

"No one wants to see that," Toad added as if trying to lighten the mood.

Conall's jaw clenched tightly, and I was convinced I could hear his back molars. I started to say it wasn't necessary, but then Conall spoke. He ran through all the events leading him to Belton: Liz, the photos, Earl's condition, Dog's treatment of him, and ended with us retrieving his things.

Sid sat silently through it all. A red hue developed over his cheekbones that didn't look healthy. "That fucking scumbag. I expected better of Dog too." He shook his head, his lip curling as if he smelled something bad. "You looking to prospect with Dark Angels? I'll support that."

Conall's mouth fell open as he stared at Sid, who was moving in his seat to face forward. Toad reached out and laid a hand on Sid's thigh in a move that looked comforting. I did the same to Conall, squeezing gently, giving him a reassuring look that everything was gonna be fine. Right then, for me, I couldn't think of a negative of Conall becoming a prospect. Fuck no.

Calliope danced back out of her bedroom, clutching several pieces of clothing to her chest. "Nutty was nice to lend me her things, but it's so good to have something that fits." Her smile was bright, and I returned it.

"You've got several inches on her." I winked cheekily at her. "Looking like Con had shrunk your clothes in the wash wasn't a good look."

Con cuffed me over the back of the head in a move that was so natural I stilled as Calliope laughed. "You need to be careful, Con. Beatin' up the landlord could get us kicked out." As if she'd realized what she'd said, her cheeks paled, and Conall stopped mid-stride between the kitchen counter and the couch.

He cast a quick glance at me, his gaze assessing. I shook my head. "I'd never kick you guys out. Maybe we should talk about this fully."

A lot had happened since the visit to Linc's. With the full story, Sid had gone off on Linc for keeping secrets. Linc had let Sid rant, then put him in his place, explaining he hadn't had enough time to do more than scratch his ass after returning from his trip to Vegas. That cooled Sid's jets, and that was when he'd brought up Conall becoming a prospect.

Conall had kept quiet through the conversation until Linc asked if he was interested in Dark Angels and told him what was required to become a member. With Calliope out in the yard with River, he'd asked if he could talk to Calliope first. Which made the level of attraction to him creep up by another notch with how he wasn't making decisions that would affect Calliope too. Then Sid had gone one step further and offered Conall a job at the auto shop. Conall had met this with wide-eyed shock. Something else for him to think on.

Now we were back at my apartment, and I had a gut that was being attacked by nerves over the way the conversation was gonna go. Conall nodded while Calliope padded over to the couch and perched on the edge of the cushion, clutching her clothes to her chest.

The uncertainty in her eyes made my heart ache. Conall moved slower and sat beside her, slinging an arm around her shoulders. "Could you be happy in Belton?" Con asked quietly, looking directly at his sister.

I held my breath, waiting for her answer.

"I think so. I ain't been anywhere except here and River's home. It looks like a nice place. The folks seem friendly. It ain't like we got a ton of options, do we?"

"We do. We don't have to stay if you don't want. We can go any place you want. Start over."

Eyes that were far too old held Conall's gaze. "Ya think? Is running the answer?" She was so grown up. It hurt that some fucker couldn't keep his dick in his pants and wouldn't take no for an answer, taking her childhood from her.

"What do you want, Calliope?" I asked, crouching in front of her.

"I want to feel safe," she whispered, but she might as well have shouted from the apartment roof. The impact nearly knocked me on my ass.

There was a hissed curse from Conall, but I kept my gaze on Calliope and offered my hand. Hers slid into mine, cool and soft. "Do you feel safe here?"

The nod was immediate and stalled the acceleration of my pulse. "Do you want to stay here with Conall and me?"

She glanced at her brother. "Yes. I don't want to run. We did nothing wrong. Mason said he'll help us, and I trust him." She turned back to face me. "I trust you."

That, for me, was all that mattered right then. I nodded. "Okay. Then I'm gonna suggest we give this living all together a three-month trial and see how,"—I finally met Conall's dark, brooding stare—"we all fit. Does that work for you both?"

The seconds ticked by as Calliope and I waited for Conall to answer. The need for air when he nodded made me sound like a train puffing, but I was too relieved to care. "Cool, now that's decided. Who wants to watch a movie and eat popcorn?"

Chapter Fifteen

Conall

"What do you mean?" I stared at Mason, trying to comprehend what he was saying. I'd handed over all the paperwork I'd found in the trailer to him on Monday when he'd reminded Kyle to get me to drop it off. That had been two days ago, and then he'd called this morning asking me to come to his office alone, I hadn't known what to expect.

Having never stepped foot in a lawyer's office before, I had nothing to compare the swank office with the air of expensive smells and furniture that looked to cost big bucks. He eased back in his office chair. His dark-gray suit was classy and gave him an air of polish that didn't fit with who his boyfriend was. If I hadn't seen Mason with Linc, I'd never have put the two of them together.

He steepled his fingers under his chin, wearing a thoughtful expression. "I mean that your mother never gave legal guardianship to Earl. He has no claim over Calliope. In fact, the trailer, what's in it, and whatever money she has in her

account were all left to you and Calliope. As Calliope's
blood relative, you have legal guardianship of her." He was
as cool as a damn cucumber.

What he said made my stomach burn with yet more regret. The agitation was too much to sit still as the reality
of the situation crashed over me. Another wall of bricks
crushing me with what I'd allowed to happen. Life was a
real fucking shit pit.

Standing, I paced in front of Mason's office desk. I barely
noticed the view out the window of Killeen, with the turmoil churning in my gut. "What you're sayin'? We didn't
have to put up with his crap all this time? And that motherfucker knew? Knew he was taking us for a ride?"

My hands fisted at my sides, the nails biting into my
palms. The bite of pain was not nearly enough to stop my
head from whirling with this recent change of events.

Mason's brows rose and then merged. "I don't know
what your mother did or didn't discuss with Earl. And
it's pointless guessing at something we'll never know." He
came forward and tapped the crumpled papers in front of
him. "This is a good thing, Conall. It means you won't have
to go to court."

"Great," I growled, running my shaking hands through my
hair at how my assumptions had left Calliope vulnerable. I
stomped once more in front of his desk. "That doesn't mean
I can magically go back and kick the fucker out of our home,
does it? Stop what he did to Calli. No, it means I once again

let my little sis down by not bothering to check what the lying scumbag was sayin'."

"Have you finished having your pity party?" The snap of Mason's voice and the question brought me to a standstill.

I eyed him over the desk, my anger spoiling for a target. I sucked in a deep breath, then another, reminding myself Mason was doing me a favor and that this wasn't his fault. "Sorry," I mumbled, and flung myself dejectedly back in the seat.

"I get your anger. I'd feel the same in your position. But right now, focusing on things you can't change isn't gonna help Calliope or you." He tapped the paperwork again. "From the bank paperwork, there is money in your mother's account. All the information is in here to close it and transfer the money to another account of your choosing. This should have happened when she died. By Earl not doing this, which we know he couldn't, he's been illegally defrauding you and breaking several federal banking laws. Something else to add to the list of crimes to pin on him."

The smile that appeared gave me cause to reevaluate Mason. Dangerous was what sprung to mind as he continued. "I've reconsidered that with this information, it's in your best interests to contact the police department in Round Rock. They'll be aware that it's your home and need to inform you that a crime has happened there. I'm surprised they haven't made more effort to contact you."

He shook his head. "Anyway, I think we should do it now. Then you can decide where to transfer the money and what, if anything, you want to do with the trailer. We might as well get all that worked out, so that when Earl wakes up"—Mason's white teeth appeared in a feral smile—"he's left with nothing of yours."

I couldn't swallow past my dry throat. It took several attempts to get my throat to work. "Where do you think I should start?"

"The call to the police department first." His hand was already reaching for the phone, so I kept quiet as he got his secretary to contact them, then transfer the call to us.

"Round Rock Police Department, Officer Franklin, how can I help?" came a deep male voice.

"Good morning. I'm Mason Davenport, a lawyer from Killeen. I have a client, Conall Regan, with me. He's received a call to inform him there was an incident in his trailer in Round Rock and that his stepfather, Earl Levitt, was attacked and is in the hospital. Are you dealing with this case?"

"Mr. Davenport, yes, I'm dealing with the case." The caution came over loud and clear.

Mason was a skilled storyteller, keeping it close to the truth as he explained what he was interested in and who Officer Franklin needed to contact to verify who Mason was. That took a couple of minutes, and when the officer was back on the line, he sounded majorly pissed.

"Now, shall we get down to business? Mr. Regan is with me now, as you can imagine, he's very concerned about this situation. As soon as he found out, he came to see me."

"Why would he come to see you? He got something to hide?" he sneered. "Surely, if Mr. Regan was so concerned, he would have returned to Round Rock?"

"My client has nothing to be concerned about in relation to this incident." The lawyerly tone was snooty and more than a little condescending, and I enjoyed the show. "He came to me because of his prior dealings with the police department in Round Rock. *I'm sure you understand his concerns.*"

A loud snort got an eye roll from Mason, who continued on like the other man wasn't being disrespectful. I was used to it. We had a well-deserved bad rep.

"Your client is a member of Chosen Few along with the assaulted victim. I'm sure *you understand* we need to speak to your client in person regarding the attack. We have been searching for Mr. Regan for the past couple of weeks to inform him that his stepfather is in the hospital in critical condition. *His friends* didn't know where he was or his contact number."

Mason once more shook his head when I went to speak. "Understandable under the circumstances. Now can we move on? Mr. Regan left Round Rock with his sister because he obtained a job working in Belton due to a lack of opportunities for him in Round Rock. It therefore makes it hard right now for him to come back there. Please, can you clarify what requires a visit in person when we can surely answer any of your questions over the phone? Unless you are required to formally question him?"

"No," Officer Franklin spat out.

"Well then, we don't wish to add any delays to your investigation. Do you have any leads? Witnesses that can assist with finding who did this?"

"This is an ongoing investigation, and I'm unable to share any information at this time."

They had nothing. If they did, they'd have been on me like flies on shit. I'd been pulled a time or two. Or it was because they couldn't give a rat's ass that a member of Chosen Few was in the hospital. It could be either. The contempt from the cops became more obvious with each visit they paid us. "Then what do you wanna ask me? 'Cause I know shit."

Half an hour later, Mason hung up, and I had a line of sweat down the middle of my back. My T-shirt clung uncomfortably to my skin as I eyed Mason with new respect. He'd kept the questions solely related to the attack. "Do you think they believed me?"

"Debatable, but I'd say that's more to do with their bias toward the motorcycle club than any evidence they've got."

He jotted something down on the legal pad in front of him as he continued, "From what I gleaned from reading between the lines, Earl's condition has improved, and they are relying on him being able to tell them who did this." His gaze came up to meet mine. "Will Earl tell them it was you?"

That was the big question. A brother that rated out another was a big deal and would see Earl getting booted out of the chapter. The problem was, with Dog standing by Earl initially and their long-term friendship, I wasn't sure how it would or could go down.

"Don't know. Brother code is scared, but what he did crosses a huge line." I scratched at my bristly jaw, looking out at the bright sunny day beyond the window, feeling nothing but cool dread curl in my stomach. "I need to talk to Dog properly. Clear the air."

"Do you want to go back to Round Rock?" Nothing in his voice said he had any thoughts on that.

"Nah, I ain't never going back. I'm done with them. If you can't trust a brother, you've got fuck-all."

He nodded. I wasn't sure what Linc had shared with him, but he seemed clued-in with club rules. "Okay, then, do you want me to process the bank details and get that set up? I can organize the sale of the trailer as well. The officer kindly advised it's no longer part of their investigations."

"The bank stuff, is there much in there worth transferring?" I'd been too angry earlier to ask. Mom didn't have much of anything that I was aware of.

He shuffled some papers. "Twenty-six thousand four hundred dollars and ninety-one cents."

I choked on the spit I'd just swallowed, eyes widening as I stared at Mason. "How can that be? She had nothing."

Thumbing through the sheets, his gaze narrowed. "Looks like she might have had a life assurance policy." When he looked up, there was anger sparking in his eyes. "It was initially fifty thousand. It looks like Earl has spent half of it, but it was meant to be shared."

"Cocksucker!" I wasn't sure what to make of it all when, some months, things had been real tight, and I'd had to borrow from my brothers to pay for food. The fucker knew this too.

"Yes, so it would seem." He picked up the phone once more. "Linda, could you bring us some coffee and your notepad?"

When she agreed, he put down the phone, and the dangerous smile was back. "Let's cut the fucker off at the knees legally."

Chapter Sixteen

Kyle

I had an ache in the upper left-hand side of my back from the position I'd been in doing the last tattoo. I rolled my shoulders and stretched out as I ambled down the stairs to check what my work day was like the next day. Thursday's could be a little slower, and I was hoping this was the case as I wanted to leave early, so I could suggest going to Hardie's drive-in theater as they were screening *Top Gun Maverick*, a movie Calliope had said she'd like to see. Seeing as Thursday wasn't like a Friday or Saturday date night thing, I hoped to persuade Conall to join us.

He'd kept his distance since I'd held his hand. Was I pushing too hard... probably? This was me, and I wasn't sure how else to behave after he'd pointed out I wasn't being me. When I wanted something, I went after it.

"What's the pouty mouth for?" Troy asked as I stopped at the reception desk. Nutty was nowhere in sight.

"Am I pouting?" I answered, distracted by Troy leaning over the desk and grabbing what looked like a compact mirror.

He flicked the thing toward me. "See." Before I could look, he dropped the mirror down on the counter, making it clatter. "What's with you? First, the weird clothes for weeks." His gaze skimmed back down my usual attire. "Now you're back to being you. Did I miss somethin'?"

Glancing about the reception area, seeing it was empty, I looked back at Troy. "First, weird clothes. You can talk." I pointed to the super-skinny jeans that acted like a second skin and showed off Troy's super-skinny frame. "Those things look like they're trying to become part of your body."

Shaggy blond hair tumbled about his face, his aqua-blue eyes full of laughter. "They are, and you're jealous you ain't got the figure of a super noodle."

I chuckled at his description of himself. That was exactly what he looked like. "Super noodle, good one."

"So, what did I miss? You've been off giving everyone-don't-ask vibes, dressing like a preppy dude vomited all over you after your trip home."

The genuine concern was why I liked Troy. He was a go-with-the-flow guy who paid attention but only asked, like now, when he felt he could. It was a talent. "You know Ink, my friend from back home?" He nodded. "He set me up on a date. The dude rubbed me the wrong way. I felt inadequate."

Troy patted my shoulder.

"Anyway, I got some new clothes, thought I needed to fancy myself up."

"Change, you mean."

I blew out a breath at how he'd pinned it down as easily as Conall. "Yeah, that. Anyway, someone pointed out that if I didn't act like myself, how would others like me."

"Sensible dude, and he's right." He gave me a one-armed hug. "And just for the record, I like you."

Nutty came clomping down the stairs. Her biker boots hit mid-calf, and her dress hit mid-thigh, revealing a lot of leg. She bounced toward us, black dress swirling around her legs. "What's not to like about Kyle?" Spiked bangs and makeup that gave her a smoky eye completed the look.

"You got a hot date?" Troy let me go to lean against the reception desk.

She gave him a flirty smile. "Maybe." She glanced at me. "Did you need something?"

"No, I just wanted to check what I've got booked for tomorrow. I was hoping to take Calliope and Conall to the drive-in tomorrow. They're showing *Top Gun Maverick*."

"I didn't know that? And who are Calliope and Conall? I don't think you've mentioned them before."

"I haven't," I smirked and walked around the counter to look at the schedule. "They're new friends. Conall was a member of Chosen Few."

"No messing up my stuff," Nutty reprimanded, snatching the schedule out of my hand before she flipped it open and ran a blood-red nail down my column, listing off everything I had booked for the next day.

"Great." I grinned at the pair.

"Want company tomorrow?" Troy asked as Nutty tucked the schedule back in place and came back around the counter, going straight for the door.

"Erm…"

Nutty gave us both a little wave and disappeared out the door, muttering something I didn't hear.

"Well?" He gave me such a hopeful look I didn't have the heart to say no.

"If you're free, then yeah, why not."

On my way home, I'd kicked myself about ten times, but there was little I could do about it now. Then I wasted time trying to come up with a way to ask Conall and Calli without sounding lame. But there was something seriously wrong with Conall when I got home. I was getting a read on his moods, and his expression didn't say pissed but majorly upset. And whatever it was, he was keeping it to himself.

I'd tried twice to get him to talk, and okay, we didn't have a long-term friendship where we were used to sharing all our shit, but I'd hoped we'd gotten past the awkward silences. Like the one we had going on now as he helped me make dinner. I'd hoped to use the time to broach the subject of going out. That hadn't happened because I wasn't sure what had caused him to be upset. Was it me?

I didn't think so.

From the way Calliope spoke, Conall hadn't gotten home long before me. Had he been in Killeen with Mason all day? Linc had mentioned Mason had gone through the paperwork, and there were some things he urgently needed to talk to Conall about. Was that why I was getting the cold shoulder and grunted replies?

"You finished grating the cheese?" I nudged Conall's shoulder, giving him my biggest smile.

Wordlessly, he passed the bowl to me. When I took it, he walked to the sink with the cheese grater and rinsed it under the tap.

Calliope, who'd been curled up in the large seat I'd dragged over next to the window where she'd earlier sat on a dining chair that hadn't looked comfortable, strolled over, her flip-flops slapping against the soles of her feet.

She leaned on the counter, her hair hanging loosely around her shoulders. Her baggy T-shirt had a large rainbow on it, making her look younger than her fourteen years because it hid her curves. One brow rose as she titled her head in Conall's direction and mouthed, "What's up with him?"

I shrugged. "No clue," I mouthed back.

My gaze went back to Conall, who turned and glanced at us, a frown pinching his brow. "What?"

"You're in a mood. Why?" Calliope's direct approach got a wince.

"Sorry...I..." He dragged wet hands through his hair, a move I'd seen him make when he got agitated about something, but not when they were dripping water. He didn't seem to notice drops trickling down the sides of his face.

Fuck, it must be bad!

The lost look in his eyes was hard to resist. My fingers tightened on the spoon I was using to stir the mac and cheese. "Is it something I can help with?"

His shoulders sagged, and something akin to defeat stared back at me. "No. Mason has handled what he can today." His hands were back to running through his hair as he stared at his sister. "We don't got nothin' to worry about. Regarding legal guardianship, Earl never had no rights over you."

Oh fuck. It didn't take a genius to figure out that Conall was blaming himself for not knowing. Or getting his sister out of harm's way sooner. He never shied away from what he saw as his own responsibilities. It was what I really liked about him. This had to have struck deep. When he walked to Calliope, I got the sense there was more.

"Mom had insurance that paid out fifty grand, and the trailer belongs to us, not Earl." He slipped his arm around her shoulders and hugged her to him in a way that suggested he really needed touch.

His gaze met mine over her head. The devastation was hard to cope with when Calliope spoke, "Earl spent the money, didn't he?"

"Half of it. Mason is doing what Earl should have done when Mom died and making sure we get the rest."

The scent of burning cheese forced me to look away and pay attention to what I was doing. I stirred the pot, trying to save the meal while I listened to the conversation like an interloper.

"Does that mean you'll want to move out of Kyle's?"

My head twisted as I lifted the pot off the heat, desperate for the answer, but not if Conall was going to say yes. The devastation from moments ago was replaced by something not so easy to read. A solid lump formed right in the middle of my chest when he held my stare.

"That's up to Kyle. It's gonna take a few weeks to figure out the legal stuff, and I'm selling the trailer, not that I think we'll get much, but it would help to pay rent on a place."

"Is that what you want?" *Say no, please say no.*

Calliope answered first. "I don't wanna move. Kyle said we could stay."

Conall nodded. Something flickered in his gaze before it dropped, and he kissed the top of Calliope's head. "It has to be Kyle's choice."

That was easy. "I told you both already. I'm happy for you to stay as long as you want to. There's plenty of room." I placed the pot on the side and came around to get closer to the pair. "You clean." I flicked the end of Calliope's nose playfully and mock whispered, "And you don't leave your underwear hangin' in the bathroom."

She giggled like I'd hoped and eased a little of the tension in the room.

"Are you sure?" This came from Conall.

"Absolutely. Now, who wants burned mac and cheese?"

Chapter Seventeen

Conall

We slipped into a routine so easily I kept waiting for the other shoe to drop. Kyle was as laid-back as anyone I'd known, and that appeared to be his normal. Nothing seemed to faze him. He'd adjusted to having both of us in his space like we'd been there all the time. It was unsettling. Given nothing for free my whole life, I didn't know how to deal with what was happening. After the conversation last week and Calli saying she wanted to stay, I'd brought up paying rent again. Mason was still dealing with the money situation, so what I had taken from Earl and what little I'd put by was paying for the counseling Liz had arranged. Kyle had insisted it was the priority, leaving me owing him big time.

Hard-headed fucker. He'd been adamant that until I started working and helped Calli with everything she needed, he wasn't gonna take a red cent from me. We'd argued, but I'd have had more luck talking to a wall. I'd let it drop for now, but we'd be revisiting it as soon as I got the money owed or a paycheck, whichever came first. A paycheck looked more likely if I didn't fuck up at the auto shop.

Nerves fluttered in my gut at how clueless I was about what Sid would want me doing, but he'd been sure he'd come up with something useful. I hoped to fuck he was right.

"What time are you heading to Stone's?" Kyle called from across the room, where he was fiddling with what appeared to be a toaster in pieces that he'd scattered on the table.

I looked at my bare feet. Hadn't I been quiet? "In twenty. I'm droppin' Calli off at school first."

"Fuck," Kyle scowled, then sucked his thumb in his mouth, finally looking up.

"Problem?" I inquired, seeing he wasn't cursing me, but what he'd been messing with. The last few days had been much like walking on eggshells when it came to the unmistakable heat level between us. Heat Calli had pointed out after the non-date date to the drive-in with Calli and *Troy*.

The vibe the dude gave off suggested he was gay. He was very touchy with Kyle, who didn't seem to notice. And yeah, the guy seemed genuine enough, friendly, and chatted to Calli like they were long-lost friends. But I'd watched him closely when he'd slung his arm over the back seat and gotten a little too close to Kyle for my liking. I was told the movie was great, but I'd paid more attention to what Troy was doing with Kyle. Granted, it hadn't been much. But my head couldn't get past the fact only days earlier, Kyle had held my hand.

When Calliope had cornered me after the movie, she'd stated in no uncertain terms that Kyle was a decent guy. One who wouldn't fuck with anyone's head when I couldn't keep quiet about Troy's behavior and Kyle's simple acceptance of Troy's touch.

Friends, was it as simple as that? The lack of answer kept me at a distance from Kyle. And if I'd caught Kyle looking perplexed once or twice, I'd put it down to the newness of living together as...*friends*. Friends...yeah, it didn't fit, but it was the best I could come up with.

His thumb made a popping noise coming out of his mouth, and I worked to keep my thoughts clean as he waved the wet thumb at me. "That's the second time I've trapped my damn thumb in the mechanism. The thing keeps stickin' and burning the toast, so I thought I'd take it apart and grease it, see if it would work better." The scowl deepened, making him look cuter than it should have.

Stop that. He ain't cute. "Need a hand?"

"I've already wasted too much time on it." He knocked it with his other hand, giving it a sulky pout. "If the offer stands later, then yeah." When he glanced back up, the sunny smile reappeared, this one hitting directly in my solar plexus. "I was gonna make you both first-day breakfasts. But my toaster had other ideas." He shook his head and walked over to the sink, his ass swaying and drawing my attention to how the soft denim clung to his backside.

"—so if that works, we could do that?"

"Huh?" I met Kyle's amused stare, having gotten caught and missed what he was talking about.

"Conall, when are we leavin'?" Calliope's inadvertent rescue got a chuckle from Kyle. I must have looked relieved at not having to explain that I was clueless about what he'd been talking about.

"I just need to get my boots on, then we can leave. It's a good ten-minute walk to the school." My gaze swept over her. She'd paired skinny jeans with a sloppy tie-dye sweater in a swirl of blues and greens that made her eyes stand out. Her long curls were loose around her shoulders, and it pleased me to notice the bruising was barely noticeable. The first session with the counselor Liz had recommended was this afternoon after school. We'd walked the route, so I knew she was okay finding the place. The idea of asking Sid for time off on my first day didn't seem like a great way to start, but I would have. But Calli had been insistent she needed to do this for herself.

"What time does the session with the counselor end?" Kyle questioned as he laid two brown sacks on the counter.

"Four-thirty. Are you sure you'll be free?"

I glanced between them, trying to work out what I'd missed.

"Yeah, my last client is at two because I don't normally work a Monday." He gave a casual shrug and then held out the paper sacks and wiggled them. "Lunch."

"Thanks," Calli said, taking the bag and slipping it into the new backpack I'd bought her. On her way back to me, she frowned. "Don't you want yours?"

"Huh?" Back to acting like a dork and feeling touched by his thoughtfulness, heat coursed through me faster than a blow torch melting metal.

The sound of Kyle's chuckle got my feet moving. "Great...thanks...erm, yeah, okay, see you later." I headed toward the door.

"Shoes, shoes would be good," Calli called after me, completing my morning of *look at me, I'm so together, not* dorkiness.

Making my escape to my bedroom, I heard the laughter as I shut the door and thudded my head against the wood. *Get it together, you damn fool. He's only being helpful, not sucking your fucking cock!*

The rest of the morning was a little better if I discarded the knot of apprehension right between my shoulder blades. The guys at the auto shop seemed like a decent bunch and didn't appear phased by my presence. Which made me wonder if Sid had given them a warning. The following day was the club meeting, where I'd get formally introduced to the other members of Dark Angels, and they'd decide if I could become a prospect.

I kept my worry about not being accepted to myself. Kyle appeared to think it was a foregone conclusion. But there'd be questions about what had happened with Chosen Few. I expected it, only I wasn't ready to share what had happened to Calliope with anyone else.

"So, we don't touch anything that's hot. Linc would skin you alive if you did that. So would I. It's taken years to get rid of the rep, not that it's totally gone 'cause folks have long memories, and the sheriff hates us." The gleam in Sid's eyes suggested he didn't give a rat's ass.

"No worries. I won't do anything stupid."

"Good to hear. Right, now to the paperwork." Sid's voice gave away how much he wasn't keen on that.

Sid had spent the last couple of hours showing me around and explaining what happened in the shop. Business, from what I could see, was good. Toad's area was sweet. The guy had mad skills with a paint gun and the freehand work was stunning. I could have spent hours staring at the bike he was working on. There was no way I could afford to get one of his special paint jobs, but it didn't stop me from drooling at the window display Sid proudly showed off.

In the office, I stared at the messy desk and shelves. There was paper everywhere I looked. It was as if someone had set off a bomb in the place. Dark, greasy smears covered many of the bits lying around. My hands itched to clean it up. I wasn't a neat freak—anything but—I'd just always figured that if I knew where stuff was, it was easier to find it when I needed it.

Sid didn't appear to have the same belief as he shifted piles of paper around, cursing. "Where the fuck is it? I know I printed off the forms you'd need." The scowl turned thunderous as a pile of papers scattered over the floor at my feet.

"Sid, you free for a minute? I—"

"Ram, do I look fucking free to you?" Sid waved several sheets of paper at Ram. The scowl made me step back a little to give Sid room. "Why do I have to put up with this shit?"

Seeing it wasn't a question to answer, it tempted me to swallow back my offer of help. Then I remembered I now worked for Stone's, or I would when Sid found the paperwork in this mess. "I can straighten up the office if you want?"

"If I want? Don't say stupid shit. Of course I want. If you can put some order to this, you're welcome to it." The scowl lessened, making him look a fraction less scary. "You any good with computers?"

"I know how to use one if that's what you're askin'."

His eyes narrowed on me. "What about spreadsheets?"

Ram leaned against the doorjamb, grinning. He was one of the mechanics that worked at Stone's, and he'd been friendly enough when Sid introduced us.

"I could figure them out." I spent some time on the computer at the clubhouse. I'd always enjoyed learning new things, and since I'd never been in a position to own one, I'd spent a few hours seeing what it was capable of when it was free. Any spare cash went to my motorcycle.

A buzz of excitement came when I glanced at the iMac on Sid's desk, imagining what it could do.

"Great." Sid waved his arm around the room. "This is your job. The password for the computer is Stones."

What does he mean?

Before I could ask, he walked out, and I stared at his back as Ram laughed loudly, slapping me on the shoulder. "I hope you know what you're doin'."

So the fuck do I.

Chapter Eighteen

Kyle

"Great, I'm so happy you're loving it." I nudged the dude toward the door, encouraging him toward the stairs. He'd been waxing lyrically for fifteen minutes, eating into the time I needed to go meet Calli after her therapy session. I didn't want to be late. "Let's get Nutty to schedule your next appointment for a refill on the one on your shoulder. Man, you seriously need to use sunscreen to stop the fade."

Paul gave me a sheepish grin as he finally moved a little quicker down the stairs. "Yeah, I just forget when I'm outside working."

"Then don't take your top off," I suggested, shaking my head, then turned to Nutty, who was putting the phone down. "Can you set Paul up with another appointment in six weeks?"

She flicked pages in the schedule and chewed on her lower lip. "It'll need to be eight. You ain't got any spaces before that."

It gave me a boost to think that my work was getting popular. "That'll be fine's only a touch-up." I slapped Paul on the shoulder. "See you in a couple of months."

"Cool."

Not waiting for Paul to say more, I ran back upstairs and quickly cleaned up. I'd done most of it while Paul had expressed his excitement over the new ink. Five minutes later, bag over my shoulder, I headed back down. Nutty was back on the phone, so I mouthed, "I'm out. See you tomorrow."

She winked and carried on talking. "Yes, it's five months' before he has the next available appointment."

Out the door, I went to Linc's truck, which he'd said I could borrow to pick up Calli. I tapped my fingers on the steering wheel as I drove the couple of miles to the therapist's office. As I indicated to switch lanes and park, Calli appeared in the doorway. One look at her swollen, red-rimmed eyes and my heart thudded painfully against my ribs.

Should Conall have come instead of me?

She didn't hesitate in opening the door and hopping into the cab when I pulled to a stop at the curb. Her hair hung around her face, shielding it. My head ran quickly through all my options, scared to get it wrong and make matters worse. "Wanna go back to the apartment and binge on Ben & Jerry's chocolate fudge brownie ice cream? I've heard it has magic properties."

The giggle was wet, but she nodded. "Magic ice cream. I could do with some of that."

I waited while she strapped herself in with the seatbelt before pulling into traffic. I didn't make small talk as I watched her out the corner of my eye fiddle with the strap on her backpack. Back at the apartment, I opened the door and let her go in first. Following behind, I went to the freezer and grabbed the tub and then two spoons. "Table or couch?"

"Couch." Standing beside it, she dropped her bag to the floor and plonked herself down.

"Great choice." I carried the tub and the spoons over to her and offered her one.

She eyed the tub and looked toward the kitchen area. "Nah, bowls are only for those who don't get this tub." I wiggled it in the air. "This is a one-sitting portion."

The laughter was less fragile and warmed my heart. I sat beside her and peeled off the lid, squeezing the sides to warm and melt it before offering her the ice cream. A large scoop later, she sucked on her spoon while I dug in and did the same.

The silence was easy as the tub passed between us. When she leaned against me and rested her head on my shoulder, something unfurled in the pit of my stomach. The warmth of it left me feeling a little teary. I blinked and sucked the chocolate goodness off my spoon, working on distracting myself.

"Do you think a boy would be interested in me, knowing...?"

I didn't move, certain that if I got this wrong, I'd fuck up the fragile bond between us when she didn't say more. She didn't need to. I got where she'd been leading. "Yes, I do. If I were straight and ten years younger, I'd see your inner strength.

The courage it takes to talk about something you couldn't prevent." I twisted my head and kissed the top of her head. "You're a very special girl, Calli. Don't let anyone tell you differently. What happens to us doesn't define us. It's what we make of ourselves despite the awful shit life throws our way that matters." The words hit home more than I expected because they applied to not only her but Conall and any other person who gets kicked in the gut, gets back up, dusts themselves off, and tries again.

The rattle of keys drew my gaze to the door guiltily when I eyed the nearly empty ice cream tub and remembered my promise to make a meal.

Conall eyed the tub I was holding, then his sister. The concern was immediate. He kicked the door shut with the heel of his boot. Dropping the keys on the table, he came and sat on the other side of her, wrapping an arm over her shoulder. "How you doin', kid?"

She snuggled into him but didn't pull away from me, connecting the three of us. A lump formed in my throat.

"Okay." She held up the chocolate ice cream-coated spoon. "Kyle fed me ice cream."

"The cure for everything," I joked, aiming for lightheartedness when Conall glanced over Calli's head at me. A warmth in his gaze heated my chest, making the lump grow bigger.

He gave me a small nod. "Is that so?" He eyed the remaining melted ice cream in the tub. "Then where's mine?"

Calli lifted her head, and the grin was pure mischief. "I'm sure there's enough around Kyle's mouth to satisfy you."

"Huh?" I licked my lips. The amount of chocolate I could taste on my tongue caused an embarrassed flush to fill my cheeks. I shifted away, using the back of the hand holding the spoon to swipe over my lips without thinking. A dollop of ice cream dripped onto my thigh. The brown gooiness slithered down toward the carpeted floor.

Before I could react, Conall reached over his sister and swiped at the mess, then sucked his finger into his mouth. The heat coursing through me was for a totally different reason. My mouth hung open as my body tingled with an image of what he could do with that tongue.

I gulped and looked away when the sexual tension between us crackled.

Calli giggled and got up. "I think that's my cue to go and do my homework."

"How did it go today?"

I suspected Conall wasn't asking just about starting a new school.

"It was"—Calli looked at me—"okay. Ice cream helped. Bethany, my therapist, says it'll get easier. That the first time talking about hard stuff is always the worst with a stranger."

She looked so young and fragile, yet composed as she shrugged. "I like her. She didn't push, so it felt all right to talk about it, about how I'm feeling." Another shrug, only this one was a little jerkier. Her cheeks paled before she picked up her bag and went to the kitchen to drop the spoon in the empty sink.

When she came back, she appeared a little more composed. She held up her backpack. "The school is strict on homework. And since I have a bunch to catch up on, I'm gonna make a start. Call me if you want me to lend a hand with dinner."

She disappeared in the direction of the bedrooms, then there was the sound of a door shutting.

Conall looked directly at me. "Did she say anything else? She looks like she's been crying."

"She hasn't cried since I picked her up. But yeah, she must have when she was with Bethany."

He stood and paced, the playfulness of earlier gone as he frowned. "Thanks for picking her up...being there for her."

I stood, placed the tub and spoon down, then took hold of his arm when he was within reach. "It isn't an issue, and you don't need to thank me. I wanna help any way I can."

He looked at the hand touching his arm. "Why are you really doing all this?"

The utter seriousness of his expression and the frustration in his voice made me think hard about the response, knowing he'd needed me to be honest. "Many reasons. I enjoy helping people. I hate when folks get kicked by life for no damn reason that makes sense. Calli's a brilliant girl and deserves to feel safe. To have all the teenage experiences of a girl her age without fear."

I swallowed to wet my drying mouth when he came closer. Dark hooded eyes bore into mine and set my pulse dancing to a tune it didn't know. "And 'cause I like you...not in just a platonic way. There's something about you that..."

I struggled to find the right word that didn't sound corny or stupid to him. "That tugs at something deep inside me. I felt it the first time we met. And yeah, I fucked up. I get that, and Calli made me think about that today. We don't need to make ourselves different. We just need to accept ourselves as we are. It's the only way to be truly happy."

He hit my shoe toe with his boots. His chocolate breath touched my lips as his head lowered close enough that his mouth nearly touched mine. His gaze held mine. A light danced in his eyes, setting my blood on fire. "You lookin' to date me?" The words whispered over my lips.

"Yes," I answered as he pressed his mouth firmly to mine. The kiss was all heat and fire, taking my ability to focus on anything other than the man whose arms were tugging me closer. The scent of grease mixed with my shampoo and soap rolled off Conall as he pressed closer. His solid chest muscles moved and rubbed on mine as hands roamed up my back, then headed south to my ass to take a grip.

I lifted my left leg, my thigh wrapping around Conall's hip. His semi-erect dick pushed against mine as I rolled my hips and groaned with each new flood of desire pumping through me.

I gasped for breath when his mouth traveled down my neck, nipping playfully at the skin. My head lolled to the side, giving him better access. The sting of pain came with a flood of heat to my groin. Each nip and bite drove the need to be naked to the brink of no return.

We stumbled and landed on the couch with a thud. Conall was on top of me, his knee hitting my groin. "Oomph." The air left my chest, making it hard to voice the dozen swear words circulating in my head as pain radiated down my cock to my balls.

He scrambled to get off me as Calli came running into the room. I wasn't sure who was more embarrassed as I resisted rubbing myself while blinking back the tears.

"What happened?" Calli asked, though I was positive there was humor in her tone. My watering eyes prevented me from getting a good look at her face.

"Kyle tripped," Conall muttered, offering me a hand and an apologetic smile.

"Over what?" Calli glanced down at the floor, increasing the heat that was surely making me glow like a damn flashlight.

"My own feet," I managed to say when I finally caught my breath.

"Oh." The giggles came, and then Conall, the traitor, started laughing, though he did at least smother it with his hand.

"You two aren't funny." I flounced off the couch, or I would have if my cock hadn't decided it didn't like being pressed against my fly when it throbbed like a bastard. I limped awkwardly toward the kitchen, not looking at the laughing idiots. "Seeing as I'm injured, you two can make the pizza."

The giggles continued, but the laughter stopped. "Pizza, as in from scratch?"

It was my turn to laugh at the horrified-sounding Conall. I grinned evilly at him. "Yup, from scratch. It's the least you can do for...falling on me." I finished quickly when Calli got a light of interest in her eyes when they swept between us.

Calli dragged Con with her to the kitchen. "Come on. It'll be fun."

"Yeah, like gouging my eyes out."

I sniggered and reached up to open the cupboard that stored what we'd need. "We'll save the gouging until after we've made the pizza. You'll need your eyes."

"Funny fucker."

I nudged his elbow while passing and whispered in his ear, "My cock thinks so."

He made a choking sound at the back of his throat as Calli stopped sorting through what I'd pulled out. Her eyes narrowed on us. "I'm on to you two. Now stop messing around. I want to try making pizza."

"I thought you had homework to do?"

She eyed Conall like he'd lost his marbles. "Duh, pizza."

Laughing, I came around and stood next to Calliope and slung my arm over her shoulder, loving when she snuggled in. "Yeah, Con, pizza is king."

The warning light he cast in my direction didn't faze me in the slightest. I issued one of my own. *Bring it!*

Chapter Nineteen

Conall

The Dark Angels clubhouse was bigger and nicer than the one in Round Rock. The wooden walls gleamed in the light. People stood around drinking beer at the bar, which was placed at the far end of the large room. It was set along one wall, so it used the space well and stopped the place from feeling overcrowded.

Two guys, Ram being one of them, were playing pool at a table at the opposite end of the room. Scattered about were leather couches. A couple of guys were sitting on one, looking as out of place as I felt. The lack of a patch easily identified them as new prospects.

There was no scent of smoke or weed. That was a pleasant change. I'd tried both and disliked the taste they left in my mouth. Several guys looked in my direction, but none came over as Kyle headed to the bar to get us drinks.

Tucked in a corner out of the way, Sid and Linc sat, heads close together, looking to be having a serious talk about something. The tension in the back of my neck increased. Were they talking about me? Sid appeared happy with what I'd done so far in the office, though I felt a little like a fraud. It was simple work for a paycheck that was way more than I'd expected to receive. The pay would more than support Calli and me.

Was it wrong I hadn't mentioned that to Kyle? Last night, the pizza-making resulted in laughter and a messy disaster on my part that could never be called pizza. It hadn't tasted bad. It just looked like I'd already eaten it with the mess on my plate. Kyle and Calli had thought it was hilarious, judging by how they'd laughed their asses off.

By the end of the evening, Calli acted more like her old self, making my debt to Kyle bigger than ever. There'd been no more kissing, and if Kyle was disappointed, he hadn't shown it. He'd been the one to encourage Calli to bring her homework out into the living area and do it while we watched a movie. Domesticated was how it had felt. Something I'd tried not to think too hard about because I'd liked it way more than I'd ever considered. Fuck, I'd have laughed my ass off if anyone had said they'd spent their evening making pizza and watching a movie while their kid sister was doing homework. Not that I was complaining, it's just... I wasn't used to hanging with a guy I liked without getting naked.

"You worryin' about tonight? You don't need to." Kyle appeared in front of me, holding a beer bottle.

I blushed at not noticing his approach and went with his assumption about what I was thinking. "You keep sayin' that, but your brothers might not want me when they're diggin' into why I'm here."

I'd had a text from Rattlesnake just before we'd left the apartment to say that Dog had let all the brothers know I wasn't coming back. I wasn't sure how I felt about it. The offer to wait for me to get in touch appeared to have run out, and the door was now closed.

And yes, I was the one to kick it shut. It still didn't mean I wasn't conflicted about the whole mess. Rattlesnake hadn't mentioned anything about Earl, and I hadn't messaged back, so I took that as nothing had changed.

Kyle clinked his bottle against mine. "The guys are cool. I might not spend as much time here with work and life stuff, but the brothers? They're solid. You'll see."

He'd taken but one sip of the beer when Sid shouted, "Move your sorry asses. We've got business to discuss in church."

The noise in the room increased as everyone, bar the two prospects, headed through a set of double doors I hadn't been through yet. I hesitated as Kyle nudged me in the direction of everyone else. "Should I be going in there?" I glanced back at the other two men. "They aren't coming in."

"Linc told me to bring you in to church with me." He shrugged at my questioning eyebrow lift.

He tugged my free hand and didn't give me a chance to say more. He took me into the room known as the church, where all club discussions were held. Inside, I shook off his hand, eyeing those around us to see if they'd noticed. Being gay in a motorcycle club wasn't always a good thing to admit to. That Linc and Sid were, was a good sign. That, however, didn't mean the other brothers would be as accepting of a gay outsider.

The knots in my stomach didn't loosen at the hurt Kyle didn't hide as he directed me to some seats at the back of the room and nodded to several guys as we passed, who gave me suspicious looks. Those who noticed my appearance shushed as I got the feeling something was off.

It was easier to concentrate on looking around the room and compare it to the church in Round Rock. This one smelled of leather, cologne, and beer. It was a decent size, and the wood walls were the same as the main room and glowed in the lights. Loads of leather-based chairs were scattered about in no particular order. There was a table, but they had shoved it off to one side.

A tall woman with inky black hair, the only one I'd seen besides Nutty, who'd been manning the bar, came and sat next to Kyle. She'd paired her jeans with a loose T-shirt in bold red that clung to her breasts. She eyed me with interest. I got the impression she missed nothing. "Who's your friend?"

"Conall, this is Tina. She's a ball breaker, so don't piss her off."

Raucous laughter came with a flirty wink. "I don't think he's interested in my ball-breaking ability, more yours."

I choked on the sip of beer I'd just taken as she continued to laugh, gaining more looks of interest that made me want to fidget. I worked on looking relaxed and keeping my disquiet to myself.

"You messin' with...whoever he is?" This came from an older guy who'd taken a seat in the row in front of us with a wary expression as he looked at Kyle and back at me.

Sweat dripped down the center of my back, and I shifted in the seat.

"Of course, Davey, a girl's gotta have some fun. And whoever he is, Linc invited him, so let's play nice."

"Can you shut up so we can get the fuck on with business?" came Sid's voice over the din in the room. Everyone settled until there was silence.

Linc stood, and Mason, who I hadn't seen earlier, came in from a different doorway than we'd come through with Nutty behind him. Mason went and took a seat next to the one Linc had taken at the front of the room near the table prior to getting up. Nutty sat by the door, and I suspected the door led to where River was. Nutty, besides running Linc's tattoo shop, also took care of River.

"Toad would like a word first."

"Is he givin' out more gifts?" someone shouted.

Sid got up and glared at the guy who'd spoken up. "Haven't you had enough, Beanpole?"

The guy's face lost a little of its color. "Was only kiddin', Serpent."

The guy using Sid's club name suggested the anger had hit its mark. "When you're all quite finished." Linc tapped the table. Silence returned immediately. "Toad, go ahead."

Toad's face was flushed and suggested he wasn't comfortable being the center of attention. "Thanks, Killer. Most of you know my story. And how hard it was for me until you guys became my family."

There was some tittering that didn't last long when Sid aimed a hard stare that would melt a polar cap in Alaska. "We got some new prospects looking to join tonight, and well, if they're successful in their pledges, then I'd be grateful if you wouldn't mention initially about me giving out gifts."

Kyle got a perplexed look on his face.

Someone spoke off to my left. "Why not? You could get a newbie servant." There was humor in the guy's voice.

Before I had time to see who it was, Sid was across the room and had a member by the front of their T-shirt, dragging him up off the seat. "He doesn't want a servant, and we're trying to make sure those who want to get patched aren't here for some damn freebies they'll get from my boyfriend. Got it, Handlebar?" The shake he gave the guy rattled his teeth. The sound was the only one in the room.

Sid was a mean-looking son-of-a-bitch.

"No shit, sorry, I didn't mean anything by it, Serpent."

When the guy thumped back in the seat, it became obvious how much Toad meant to Sid. He would go toe-to-toe with whoever had something to say about his boyfriend. It was a good thing to know.

Linc said nothing as Sid returned and remained standing next to Toad, who, in my opinion, was looking pretty smug.

"Finished, Toad?" Linc questioned, his voice gravelly like he'd swallowed razor blades.

The nod came before Toad returned to his seat. It dawned on me that they were talking about club business in front of me as if my jacket already had a Dark Angels patch. When I glanced in Kyle's direction, he grinned.

"Before we talk about the two new pledges we've got, I'd like to talk about a transfer member from Chosen Few. Conall, otherwise known as Runner."

Transferred member? What did that mean? I didn't need to wait long to find out as Linc continued, "Some of you may remember that Dog offered protection for River while we went to Washington. Runner came and stayed at my place to ensure nothing happened to River while I was away. You understand the trust I put in someone for River." Dark eyes swept the room and landed on me briefly before moving on. "I know we've never taken a transfer before. If you have an issue with my decision, voice it now."

"Why is Runner looking to transfer?"

I couldn't see the guy's face as he was toward the front of the room.

Linc nodded at me, his brow quirking. I got up slowly, desperate to take a drink of the beer to wet my mouth when folks twisted to look at me. It was hard to gauge the crowd's mood as I nodded at everyone. Remembering that trust here was vital, I released a breath and sucked the next one in slowly. "One brother in Chosen Few attacked my sister. It ain't a place for us no longer."

"You bringin' trouble between us and Chosen Few?" This came from a dark-haired man who looked like he worked in construction, given how he dressed.

"There won't be any trouble coming from Chosen Few over this, Matt. It's an agreed transfer. Dog knows Runner is here."

"What about the brother who attacked his sister?" This came from Davey.

I shifted uneasily, knowing this would happen but still uncertain how to reply. When Linc didn't answer, I met Davey's hard stare with one of my own. "He'll be lucky if he remembers his name. If he wakes up."

What looked like approval flashed over Davey's face before it was gone, and he nodded slowly. "That mean we're gonna have the sheriff sniffing around?"

Mason stood, his suit looking out of place among the leather and denim in the room. "I'm dealing with the legalities of the situation."

Beanpole twisted in his seat. "That means there's a chance he'll bring heat down on us."

"It means that I'm dealing with the issue *legally*. As you are all aware, if any brother has a situation that requires legal advice or help, I'll assist in any way I can. That includes your family members," Mason reaffirmed in a tone that got everyone in the room to stare at him. He had a don't-fuck-with-me expression that rivaled the one Linc was aiming at the room.

"The sheriff doesn't need much to come and stick his nose in our business. We deal with it like always." Linc's tone was one no fool would argue with.

The room quietened as I received some stares that suggested this would not be the end of the discussion but would continue outside of church.

"Next, let's discuss the two pledges who wish to become prospects."

Chapter Twenty

Kyle

Conall had locked down tight his thoughts about what had happened at the clubhouse. Since we'd ridden over on our motorcycles, there'd been no opportunity to speak about Linc's decision. I'd known something was up, but Linc hadn't told me what it was. The only clue was that he'd advised me to bring Conall into church while leaving the other potential prospects to sweat it out while we discussed them.

Back at the apartment, Conall said nothing as he got off his motorcycle, helmet dangling next to his side as he waited for me. "I didn't know what Linc was gonna do. Just so we're clear, I wasn't keeping secrets."

A frown marred his forehead. "Didn't you? You brought me into church."

Helmet off, insects buzzed and traffic noise drifted from the street. I ran a hand through my hair, eyeing Conall, trying to figure out what was on his mind. It was dark, and where we were standing didn't allow me to get a good look at his face.

"At Linc's request," I stressed. "Yup, there's a good vibe between Linc and me. Don't mistake that for him confiding in me about club shit." I shook my head. "That's all Sid and Mason now...maybe. What I'm sayin' is that Linc wouldn't talk to me before the meetin' tonight. It's just not his style, and it wouldn't make him a good president if he had loose lips, which he doesn't, to be clear. Things changed after they cleaned house, but that doesn't mean Linc didn't learn a valuable lesson about trust. He won't share Calli's secrets with the brothers. That's why Linc left it up to you to decide what you told them."

The nod was slow when it came. The street light cast shadows over his features, giving him a dark and brooding appearance.

When he walked off toward the apartment building in silence, I huffed a sigh and followed. There'd been no time to talk when I'd gotten home from work. I'd barely had time to shower and inhale the burger Calli had made for me.

At times like this, when the tension between us fizzled uncomfortably, it was like the step we'd taken forward last night disappeared. Leading me back to unsteady ground with a guy who was back to being guarded.

Fuck, I got it, but it was exhausting and kind of depressing.

"Wanna go out tomorrow night?" I didn't slap my forehead, but it was a close call when Conall swung around and stopped dead in the middle of the staircase leading up to my apartment.

The light overhead didn't hide the narrowing eyes. "What for?"

"To celebrate." I willed my leaping pulse to behave and walked up the few steps separating us, grinning widely, needing to find a way past the invisible barrier. "You ain't gonna have to spend six months jumping through hoops for other club members. That deserves a night out."

The sound of his nails running over the bristles on his jaw as he scratched didn't mask my labored breathing at the possibility he'd say no. "What have you got in mind?"

The way his gaze traveled down my body gave me a hundred and one thoughts.

I voiced none of them as I ran through the local events that Conall might be interested in. My pulse leaped at what came to mind. "You got a swimsuit?"

His head tilted to the side. "A swimsuit?"

"Yup." I kept my grin to myself at the look of confusion.

"I do, but why would I need a swimsuit in the evening?"

I tapped the side of my nose. "That's for me to know and you to find out." I grinned. "It's gonna be fun, I swear."

He didn't look convinced, not in the slightest, as I came up one more stair, bumping chests. The scent of his deodorant didn't mask his masculine scent. Too low down to look him directly in the eye, I tilted my head back, uncaring that he was looking down at me.

"Trust me." I winked at him and passed by, heading up the rest of the stairs, eager to find out if they still had tickets for an adult night at Summer Fun Waterpark.

The place opened solely to adults some evenings during the week. They had strict rules about drinking and eating. They did allow a six-pack of beer, and that was fine. I didn't want to get Conall drunk. I was more interested in getting him out of his clothes so I could see what he looked like naked.

I'd already imagined it. Conall in his swimsuit was the next best thing, and getting to rub up against all that hard, wet skin was a dream come true.

Excitement hummed through me as we strolled along. The day had felt long with two tickets for the water park purchased. Troy and Linc had given me several strange looks because I'd been hyped. My music choices reflected my cheerful mood, making Linc close his door between clients.

He wasn't a fan. Although he said it was better than listening to the crap Troy and Ali played downstairs that competed for bass noise.

My palm itched with the desire to reach out and take Conall's hand, but the memory of how he'd shaken me off the night before had me shoving my hand in the pocket of my jeans. The other clutched at the bag I'd slung over my shoulder containing towels, beer, and a few other things I'd considered we might need. Yup, condoms and lube. No one ever said it wasn't wise to be prepared. The way Conall kissed me wasn't that of a man who wasn't interested in getting down and dirty. Or I fucking hoped not.

It was cool enough for a light jacket. The sky had turned a gorgeous deep orange as the sun started to set over the lake in the distance. It sparkled and helped with the relaxed mood that settled between us.

"So, are you gonna give me a hint about where we're going?"

Back in the apartment last night, I'd expected Conall to try to weasel out the answer. The man was full of surprises and hadn't. Instead, he'd gone to talk to Calli about the events of the evening, then disappeared into his own room after poking his head around my door to say goodnight.

"Oh, you want to know now?"

The shrug was his only reply.

The look he wore was one of disinterest. His eyes said differently. I'd spent some time watching his expressions. I teased him, nudging his shoulder with mine. "Somewhere where we can get"—I lowered my voice—"up close and wet."

I felt more than saw the shiver than ran through him. His eyes hooded. "You're playin' with fire, boy." The sexy threat had heat pooling low in my groin.

"Am I now?" I got even closer to him until it was difficult to keep walking. "I'm happy to test out how hot your fire is." I flirted back, enjoying the challenge.

His hand snaked around my waist, pulling me to a stop and pressing me into the side of his body right in the middle of the pavement. His face was inches from mine, wearing a dangerous smile that lit a fuse to my cock. "Hot enough that it'll take more than that lake I can see in the distance to put out."

A shiver ran down my spine in anticipation of the threat his eyes were issuing. "We'll need to see about that."

His brow quirked up, a smug smile appearing. "That we will." He didn't remove the arm from around me. No, the smug fucker slid his hand down my ass, his fingers slipping into the back pocket of my jeans. A hot press against me burned through the denim.

He squeezed just hard enough to get me moving with him and make my cock ache.

The fucker was lethal.

Well shit! How was I supposed to walk around in a swimsuit with a fucking hard-on?

I had no answer as I directed us across the street, the hand on my ass not helping me to gain control of the desire coursing through me.

When the water park came into view, Conall chuckled. "We're going in there?"

At the sound of his amusement, I grinned. "Yup. They do adult-only nights." I wagged my brows. "Unfortunately"—I winked once more—"you have to keep your swimsuit on."

The chuckle turned into a deep belly laugh that drew the gazes of those standing in line to get inside Summer Fun Waterpark. As far as I could see, we were the only same-sex couple. Not that we were a couple... *yet.*

One thing Conall might not have figured out about me is that I was persistent when I wanted something worthy of my full attention. An art degree, then becoming a tattoo artist in a reputable shop, had received my full focus, and I'd achieved both through determination and hard work. They were things I'd wanted, and I'd been happy to work hard to get them. Relationships, yeah, I'd worked at those. Although not with the same dedication, and now I understood why. None of them had been Conall. When he smiled and focused those dark, brooding eyes on me, everything else ceased to matter.

He didn't expect good things to come his way. I could see it last night when Linc had made it easy for him to be a member of Dark Angels. Had stood for him, the same way Sid had too. I wanted to offer him everything I had. Long-term. A commitment. One that would probably scare the man at my side.

"You forget the tickets or what?"

I glanced at Conall, frowning, then at the woman at the gate we were now in front of. *Fuck!*

Heat spread up my neck as I reached into my front pocket for my phone, flicking the screen to bring up the tickets so she could scan the barcode. I didn't look at Conall, who'd removed his hand but was still close enough that I could feel him shaking with silent laughter. *Asshole!*

Conall's lips brushed my ear. *"I won't ask what you were thinking about."* He pointedly dropped his gaze to the bulge in the front of my jeans.

My lips tugged into an embarrassed smile as we walked into the water park. I led Conall to where we could get changed.

Inside, I glanced at the conceited fucker standing, arms folded next to the lockers. Matching his grin, I stepped closer until we were inches apart and I could feel the heat of his body. "We're about to get wet and wild. Let's see how *you control your body*."

Chapter Twenty-One

Conall

The air whistled over my wet skin as my ass burned as I flew down the Hipster for the seventh or eighth time. Water splashed everywhere as I landed in the pool at the bottom, blinding me long enough for Kyle to surface and drag me close for a kiss.

My heart pounded from the kiss and the exhilaration. It was a heady combination. I was positive the surrounding water sizzled with the extreme heat we were generating. His body slid fluidly against me, legs intertwining with mine, allowing all the hard bits to rub together.

The water temperature was not low enough to stop my reaction this time or any of the other times the tempting fucker had made a play for me. It was possibly the best date of my life and right up there with the most painful with how my cock throbbed at the wet skin-on-skin contact. I'd tried and failed to keep it decent for those around us in the water park. Kyle was as slippery as an eel.

By the time he released me, my lips tingled, my chest heaved, and I wasn't sure how much more I could take. The threat he'd issued outside about me controlling my body returned as he dove under the water and hands snaked around the front of my swimsuit, caressing my cock before he swam off.

I gave chase as I had done every time we'd played this game for the last couple of hours. I hadn't known what to expect and initially considered it lame to bring someone on a date to a water park. I'd revised that idea the first time Kyle had slid his body against mine.

We hadn't spent the entire time in the water. We'd had a beer between runs down the slides and chatted about more personal stuff. Halfway through the evening, it struck me how relaxed I was, and that was all because of Kyle, who seemed genuinely interested in getting to know me.

He didn't want to fuck and walk. It was a new concept, one that I... liked. Kyle was open to questions, and it was easy to get him to talk.

The glint in his eyes suggested he was enjoying himself and that he didn't push me to talk if I changed the subject added to his appeal.

If anyone was paying us any attention, I hadn't noticed. Kyle held all my interest, which wasn't hard with a wet, nearly naked, tattooed hunk lavishing his attention on me. Again, not something I was used to.

I caught hold of his ankle and dragged him back to me. He surfaced, spluttering as his eyes danced with laughter. He wiped at his face, pushing back the hair from his cheeks and forehead. Water sparkled on his eyelashes as he gave me a fiery look, grinning.

My heart thudded in time to the pulsing cock wanting to bury itself inside the tease. I dove for him, and we sank into the water, lips fused together.

Feelings, way too many to name or think too hard about, barreled around inside my chest. He clung to my shoulders, holding on to me as if he could sense the turmoil that came with them.

When my lungs screamed for air, we surfaced, gasping and panting, not letting go of each other. "You ready to leave?" I made it clear what I was asking, and the nod settled my heart rate enough to stop my hands from shaking at what would happen next.

We'd been headed for this moment, if I was honest, since he'd opened the door to me. I accepted that this wasn't just fucking. We showered separately, and I didn't look at where Kyle was as he dressed.

The sky was inky black with no stars as we exited the building along with others who were laughing and joking. Kyle and I remained silent, almost as if we didn't want to break the spell between us.

Waiting on the cab, Kyle took hold of my hand. His fingers interlaced with mine, the weight and warmth adding to the swirling emotions. I couldn't have told anyone if they'd asked how long it took to get back to Kyle's or what we talked about in the cab.

Inside the apartment, I watched as he dropped the bag containing the wet swimsuits and towels on the floor, took off his jacket, dropping it on the bag. He then bent to retrieve something from the outside pocket.

The silence inside the apartment brought the knowledge that Calliope was asleep just down the hallway when Kyle held up lube and a condom.

I groaned. The arousal that hadn't relinquished its hold completely awakened as Kyle strolled toward me, hips swaying enticingly.

"We're gonna need to be quiet." I wasn't sure if I was telling him or me. It was hard not to lose control when I touched him.

He smirked as he looped one arm around my waist. He leaned into me, his lips moving over the side of my neck. "Do I need to gag you then?"

The words weren't loud, far from it, but my pulse jumped as if he'd bellowed them. There was a challenge in his eyes when he eased back as I answered. "If I remember correctly, you're usually the noisy one."

"Let's see, shall we?" He reached up with his empty hand and cupped the back of my neck, drawing my lips to his. The kiss was nothing like I'd expected. The heat was there, but it was gentler than the others we'd shared.

His mouth teased and tempted. His tongue dipped between my parted lips, stroking, before he sucked my tongue into his mouth, loving on it like it was a cock. Panting and close to an edge I didn't want to cross so fast, I was the first to pull back.

He wore a sultry look that would test the patience of a saint, which I wasn't. I removed the hand from the back of my neck and dragged him down the hallway to his bedroom because it was farther away from Calliope's.

The fucker wore a smug expression that suggested he knew why I'd opted for the space. I wasn't going to delude myself. Keeping quiet was gonna be fucking hard. The idea I might need a gag wasn't far from the damn truth with how he tempted me.

I let go of his hand as the door closed. He toed off his sneakers and dropped the lube and condom on the bed, his hands going to the hem of his T-shirt. He yanked it off and dropped it to the floor.

The flirt was back. He ran his hands up his chest, taking hold of his nipples. His eyes hooded and the smile that I'd outlawed appeared. The full throaty moan that followed sent a trail of fire straight to my cock.

"If you haven't noticed, I love having my nipples played with." He demonstrated as I remained standing in the same spot, captivated by the man before me. My usual encounters with men didn't involve much foreplay. Get them ready so I didn't hurt them, unless they liked that, then get down to business.

Kyle, it appeared, had other ideas. The tormenting he'd done at the water park didn't seem enough. I yanked my top off and dropped it where I was standing. I toed off my boots and watched him as I undid my jeans and pushed them down my thighs, along with my underwear. He exhaled gustily as his gaze dropped to my cock.

It was as big as the rest of me. I didn't shave or wax, but I kept the hair short. I stood still, letting him look his fill. The open-mouthed groan suggested Kyle approved. His fingers played and squeezed at his nipples. He made several whimpering noises as I kicked off my jeans.

I walked slowly toward him, my cock thickening as he didn't look away. The air between us sizzled as it had done at the pool. I could feel my skin dampen with the heat building between us. It was fucking amazing considering we hadn't touched... yet.

My hands went for his belt buckle, and I opened it as I crowded him. The height difference wasn't something I noticed much when dressed. Naked, the comparison between us seemed more obvious. His head barely reached my shoulder. It was fucking hot to have a smaller partner, especially one who, if I wasn't mistaken, liked to fuck and get fucked.

"What do you like...?" I looked at the fingers still squeezing his nipples. "Besides the obvious." The rasp to my voice got another groan, or maybe it was my question. It didn't matter. My cock loved the sound.

His Adam's apple bobbed. His chest rose and dropped quickly. "I'm vers. I'm open to whatever you want as long as it's just us...*no one else.*"

The message was simple, and I nodded. It was easy to agree with. I didn't want anyone touching him besides me.

"Just us," I reiterated and got down on my knees to drag his jeans down. The cock inside bounced free and slapped at his belly, hard and thick. My ass clenched at the length. He could more than compete with me, and I was eager to see what he could do with the sizable cock that looked good enough to eat.

The veins running up the length made my tongue hum in appreciation, as did the shaved skin. Several shades lighter than the skin above his waistline, it was creamy smooth. I came forward and held his gaze as I licked the skin to test my theory on how smooth it was.

He shuddered, a drop of pre-cum forming on the tip of his bobbing cock, his eyelids fluttering. "Fuck, that feels good," he murmured in a husky voice that ramped up my need to hear him carry on talking.

I tapped his leg. "Lift." When he complied, a hand dropped to my shoulder as I got him to repeat the move, so I could remove the remaining clothes.

As I rose, I placed my arms around him, my hands cupping his ass, and lifted him clear off the ground. His cock spread pre-cum over my chest as I came to fully standing. Both hands were now on my shoulders as he looked down at me, a flush coating his skin. His eyes filled with desire.

I slowly lowered him to the floor, enjoying the feel of his skin sliding against mine. The scent of sex warmed the air. I tumbled us both onto the bed. Our mouths met, and I lost myself in the taste of him. I captured every sound he made as we rolled over the enormous bed, hands roaming, learning the contours of his body as he did the same to me.

My skin was tight like I'd overheated, and it had shrunk as the desire between us escalated beyond anything I'd experienced before. In the eight years I'd been having sex, nothing had prepared me for this. Each touch took me to extra levels of desire. This was no quickie all about relieving an itch. This would never be that. I didn't focus on why. I just let the feel and smell of Kyle surround me. *Protect me.*

My heart stuttered and I shut out the thought because I didn't want to derail what was happening. The rolling lube bottle dug into my side. I reached for it as Kyle licked a path down my chest.

His lips closed over my right nipple, and he sucked hard enough that I wasn't sure if it was pain or pleasure that followed. The heat flooding my groin said pleasure. My nipple wasn't so sure. I flicked open the bottle of lube and attempted to one-handedly coat my fingers, not wanting to stop touching Kyle.

His head came up when I stopped touching his ass because I got too frustrated at failing. He blinked as if trying to focus his eyes. "Why you stoppin'?"

He was slurring like he'd drunk a quart of whiskey. I grinned at him and held up the bottle. "I ain't stopping." I wagged the bottle in front of him. "You try opening a bottle of lube one-handed and pour it over the same fingers?"

The grin was pure sex as the cock pressing against my thigh pulsed hard enough that it caused mine to buck. Somehow, I got lube in all the right places while the teasing fucker returned to sucking my nipple, gasping and groaning around the turgid flesh.

I worked the lube around his asshole, knowing it would require patience. I was in short supply of it, with how Kyle was humping and grinding against my fingers at each stroke. The rim loosened enough to push a finger inside, and my moans got loud at the feel of his ass clasping me. It didn't take much imagination to know how it would feel when I sank inside his hot, silky sheath.

By the time I had three fingers inside him, I was sweating so much Kyle could have slipped right off me. He wasn't much better. "That's enough. Fuck, is this payback for the pool?" he growled, moving until my fingers left his ass.

He was up before I could blink and question what he was doing as he ripped open the condom and slid it down my oversensitive cock. All we'd done had me ready to blow. The throbbing arousal and need to come was like a herd of raging bulls all charging at me from different directions.

The fucker stroking my cock was clearly unaware of how close I was to blowing my load. Instead of just getting the condom on me, he stroked down my length and cupped my sac, rolling my balls in his palms. He squeezed firmly, but not hard enough to stop the need to come.

Gritting my teeth, my eyelids slammed shut, then reopened barely a second later when it only made the feel of his fingers playing with my cock and balls all the more present in my mind.

"If you want me to come in your ass, then get that ass sitting on my cock...now," I rasped past my dry throat.

The chuckle was pure evil as he slung his leg over my hips. He rose, a string of pre-cum suspended between us as he reached behind him and took hold of my cock at the base, and angled it. Before the air had left my lungs and I could contend with the heat of his hole against the head of my cock, he sank down in one swift move.

"Holyyyyyyy fuckkkk," I cried out through gritted teeth.

His ass did the best impression of a compression sock on my dick. The bold move was too much, and my hips bucked as I reached to take hold of his hips in a punishing grip to keep him still and let me catch my damn breath.

But the evil fucker wasn't interested in holding still. His thighs clenched, as did his ass, and I could feel everything as he reversed, then slammed back down. The slap didn't mask his or my groan. The wildness of his moves was irresistible. I barely had the wherewithal to grab a pillow and bite the edge to stop myself from calling out. Wave after wave of intense pleasure spread through me, stealing any memories I might have had of any other sexual encounter. All I knew was Kyle. He was the beginning, the middle, and the damn end, and I never wanted it to stop.

His bouncing cock slapped against his body as mine throbbed hard in a way that suggested I wouldn't last much longer. I reached out, scooped up the precum on my skin, and used it as a lubricant.

"Fuck, yeah, that...oh god, Con, feels so good." He mewled, his head rolling forward, and he braced his hands on my slick, heaving chest. His eyes were barely open. His lips parted, and he panted, groaned, and moaned as his cock thickened and white spurts of cum pelted my chest and neck.

The tight sheath of his ass held my cock prisoner, and I bit harder at the pillow, cum filling the condom as he collapsed forward, dislodging my hand as he landed on my chest hard enough to wind me if I hadn't already been struggling to breathe.

My cock continued to pump cum into the condom as his breath tickled my damp skin for long seconds.

My eyes drifted closed, and my teeth let go of the edge of the pillow when the ache registered in my jaw.

Kyle snuggled into my sticky chest, one hand reaching for mine. Our fingers intertwined, and he made a snuffling, contented noise that a second later turned to a soft snore. My fingers squeezed his, and I considered moving to get us cleaned up...

Chapter Twenty-Two

Kyle

This morning, when I'd woken with dried cum all over me, my ass speaking to how enthusiastically I'd ridden Conall, I wasn't sure what to feel: mortified or smug? I'd come so hard I'd passed out. Or that's how it appeared when I had no memory after collapsing against Conall.

Conall, the asshole, had let me shower first. He suggested I take one alone because Calli was up and moving around. The fucker acted like the entire building heard me because I'd gotten that vocal. The flush didn't budge from my face because I was damn sure he was right. Why couldn't I be quiet? And why hadn't I suggested he go first? Was this trial by fire with Calli?

Calli grinned at me in that knowing way a teenager had that left no doubt she'd heard us making out. Never having had a sister to worry about, I was desperately trying to figure out what, if anything, I should be saying. I pulled out things to make packed lunches for everyone, doing my best to act like there was nothing to see.

Calli didn't pretend interest in the bowl of cereal in front of her. No, she kept those dancing eyes directed right at me. I could feel them watching my every move.

Why hadn't I had the same wherewithal Con had to bite down on a pillow when he'd gotten more than a little vocal? He'd cheated. That's what he'd done by shoving the pillow in his mouth. Had the fucker offered me one? Said, "Kyle, here, bite this," no! He'd left my ass hanging out in the wind, and now I had to face his sister alone.

It was all his fault if we'd... god, had I traumatized her?

I met Calli's stare properly for the first time since entering the room. She didn't look like we'd traumatized her. She smiled. That had to be good, right?

I chewed on my lower lip, working on how to ask without making the situation worse. I coughed and went back to filling the paper sacks for lunch. "Erm...last night..." I blew out a breath when I caught her arching her brows. "Did we, erm...wake you?"

"Wake me?" The innocent look didn't fly with me because her eyes didn't hide her amusement.

"Never mind." She clearly wasn't upset, and I was embarrassed enough to keep on this track. "What time is the therapy session ending today?"

Her amusement fled, and I cursed silently for being the one to bring back the unwanted reminder. "A little later than Monday, but it's cool. Con is going to come and get me."

I nodded, trying to think of a way to distract her while I continued what I was doing. "You interested in getting to know Belton? There's a great place, Stillhouse Lake, that offers a wide range of things to do on the weekends. Do you enjoy swimming? Sailing? Water sports?"

She perked up. "I enjoy swimming. The others I've never done. There wasn't much extra cash to do stuff like that." The simple shrug didn't say one way or another whether that bothered her.

"Want to do something this weekend? It'll have to be on Sunday because I have a full client list on Saturday."

"Yeah, do you think River might wanna come with us?"

I nodded. "Let me ask Linc. I know Mason has taken her out on the lake, and she'd loved it. Maybe we could have a picnic as well. Talk your brother into joining us," I said the last loud enough for Con to hear.

He appeared looking sexy as fuck. He'd brushed the damp hair back off his face. He'd left the stubble on his jaw. The T-shirt hugged the wide expanse of his chest as he shoved it into the front of the band of his jeans as he walked barefoot toward us. "What you wanna talk me into doin'?"

Calli twisted in her seat to glance at her brother. "Kyle was asking if I wanted to go to the lake for a picnic on Sunday. Maybe try some water sports. Can we afford it?"

That it was the first question had my gut clenching, and I looked at Con to see if I'd caused an issue. Liz had mentioned just how much the therapy sessions were. Con would get health insurance working for Linc, but it wouldn't cover Calli's therapy. I was pretty sure the money situation from his mom was still unresolved.

"Yeah, in fact, it'll be my treat."

Frowning, I swallowed back the retort that he didn't need to pay when he gave me a look that suggested I'd piss him off if I voiced it aloud.

Calli bounced off her seat and wrapped her arms around Con's middle. "I'm gonna ask if River wants to come too. Is that okay?"

He ran a hand over her blonde curls, smiling at her. "Yup, now don't you think you should get a move on, or you'll be late."

Back at the counter, she picked up her spoon and ate the congealed cereal. Con came around the counter and hesitated. He glanced at Calli, and I remained still, waiting to see what he'd do next, not wanting to push him.

He came closer, and I let go of the breath I'd been holding when he lowered to press a kiss on my lips before grabbing a coffee cup I'd left on the side for him.

Calli giggled but said nothing, although she watched us both as she continued to eat her breakfast.

It felt very domesticated as we moved around the kitchen. Conall ate a piece of toast while leaning against the counter.

"How was last night?" Calli finally asked, her lips twitching when Con looked at me.

"It was...energetic."

I blushed at the meaning behind his words. I thrust his lunch at him and gave him a warning stare. "We could go to the water park one weekend if you'd like. It's lots of fun, Calli."

Con's chuckle became muffled in the cup as he brought it to his lips, taking hold of his lunch sack. His eyes twinkled in a way that made my pulse leap.

"Yeah, let's hope I have as much fun as you two." With that she stood, taking the empty bowl to the sink. She winked at me and grinned at Con, who was no longer looking as amused.

I waited till she left the room before I turned an accusing stare at Con. "You could have given me a pillow to bite."

He'd never full-on laughed before, or not that I'd heard. It was a deep, rumbly sound that filled the room.

"I'm not finding it funny," I muttered, sounding way more amused than I wanted.

He placed the cup and sack down purposefully, then tugged me into his arms. His mouth nuzzled along my jawline to my ear, where he whispered, "Maybe I can make it up to you later..."

I groaned as he bit my neck hard enough to feel it and make me tingle but not deep enough to mark my skin. "How?" I managed past my tight throat when he continued to nip his way down to the neck of my T-shirt.

"I'll leave you to think about that." He let me go after another playful nip, then strolled toward the bedroom.

"Tease," I called after him.

"Only with you."

He didn't glance back at me, and I was glad as I shuddered and fanned my face at the depth of sincerity in his voice. Well, wasn't that a turn-on and just the most fucking amazing thing anyone had ever said to me?

At work an hour later, I was still thinking about it as I set up my workstation for my first client. The door swung open, and Mason appeared. "Do you have a minute?"

Dressed for work in a suit and tie, he stepped into the room at my nod. I didn't let the thoughts jumping around my head take over about whether Dog or the police department had been in touch. Jumping the gun at losing what was starting between Con and me wasn't what I wanted to think about.

I continued to pull out the inks and lay what I needed on the counter as Mason didn't immediately talk but roamed around my room.

When he looked at me, he wore a serious expression. "I've gotten to know you, and I hope you won't see this as overstepping."

The clenching in my stomach churned my breakfast as I stopped what I was doing to look at him.

"When I met Linc, I could see his past had left its mark on him. Conall wears the same marks."

I nodded. "He does. I thought about it when I first met Con, how much he reminded me of Linc. Are you here to warm me off? Tell me he's trouble?" I kept control of my emotions because if he was, then he was plum out of luck!

"No." He rubbed his smooth jaw, settling a little of the tension holding my shoulders hostage. "That's not why I'm here. Conall comes across like he's tough, both inside and out. He's not. What he might have to face needs someone who'll stand by him and his sister."

I bristled. "Are you sayin' I'm not that person? 'Cause if you are, you couldn't be more wrong. I like Conall... *a lot,* and it's not a temporary thing. Let's get that straight. As for Calli, I'm here for her one hundred percent, with or without my feelings for Conall."

The smile that followed confused the heck out of me. Mason hugged me, causing me to blink rapidly at him when he stepped back, looking very pleased with himself. "Good. Now that's cleared up, what was Nutty saying about Sunday and a picnic with Calli, Con, and you? Maybe we can all go because I've already booked a boat for the weekend at Stillhouse Lake."

Chapter Twenty-Three

Conall

It was plain weird, and I couldn't get my head to think any differently as I walked with Mason, Linc, Kyle, and the girls toward the sparkling lake in the distance, carrying a large basket full of food Mason had prepared. Linc was smiling in a way that made Mason stop in the middle of the street to kiss him.

Sunlight gleamed off their dark heads as hands roamed in a way that suggested things could get hotter than the sun beaming down on them.

Kyle chuckled as we passed the two men, and I averted my eyes, not needing to see that. Although it was hard not to see myself in Linc and what he had with Mason. Was this an alternative universe where folks like me and Linc got to have a happy ever after?

My gut fluttered with how that might not be the case with the missed call and subsequent message left on my voicemail from the Round Rock police department, asking me to contact them at my earliest convenience. Not wanting to spoil the day, I'd kept it to myself and used Calli's excitement as a distraction.

Her excitement made my chest tighten with how it was easy to compare her past life with her current one. Calli nor River paid anyone any attention as they raced ahead, chatting like two magpies. The age difference didn't seem to matter to either of them. They'd been as happy as two clams since we'd arrived at Linc's home and gathered everything for a day at the lake.

It was all so... *domesticated*.

Did I like it? Not a word I'd ever apply to myself or to the man who was president of a badass motorcycle chapter. Yet, I couldn't deny it fit, and having never really had that, I conceded to myself I liked the feelings that came with it. I wasn't sure I'd admit it aloud to my new brothers in Dark Angels or those in Chosen Few who deemed me worthy of talking to.

The definite lack of contact suggested I wasn't worthy when the only brother who'd remained in touch was Rattlesnake. It was something I wasn't dwelling on. It was pointless when I couldn't change it. The nagging feeling of never quite fitting in proved to be the case. One I'd avoided admitting to myself when it was as if I didn't always fit in my skin, not the same as everyone else.

Here it was different, and fuck if I wanted to think too closely on the why of that. Ram and a few of the others from Dark Angels had invited me out for a beer the night before after work. I'd been undecided. Then Kyle encouraged me to go. No drama as he and Calli had laid on the couch together with plans to binge-watch *Valhalla* and eat a ton of popcorn. Calli had giggled while pointing out they didn't need me bitching about the poor acting.

I'd gone, but all I could concentrate on was how my sister was happy. The genuine kind, the type I could feel deep inside when she smiled at me. Kyle wore the same smile when he looked at me. And that was harder to ignore when I was selfish and wanted to be the only one he looked at like that.

Was I the one making him that happy or was it Calli? Or both of us?

The warm fingers clinging to mine lifted, and Kyle pressed a kiss to the tips of my fingers. "You okay?"

It spoke to the man that he sensed I'd gotten lost in my own thoughts. But it was the light kiss on my fingertips that caused my heart to knock against my ribs. Such a small gesture, yet it touched my heart, making it quiver. "Just got some things on my mind," I answered truthfully.

"Talk to me." He kissed my fingers again and dropped our hands back down, continuing to walk slowly, looking at me sideways.

"Are you serious...about me and you?" For some reason, it was the first thing that came out of my mouth.

He didn't answer immediately, and I appreciated he was thinking about the reply, although my shoulders didn't because the muscles protested being held in one place for too long.

His chest rose and fell slowly. "Yes." His thumb rubbed over my fingers. "The first time we met, there was something about you that instantly attracted me." He nudged my elbow with his. "And yeah, it was physical, but it wasn't just that. Something in your eyes held me captive, and I wasn't in the least bit worried about getting away. I thought a lot and dreamed even more about your eyes. Then you turned up at Linc's door and made a dream come true."

He laughed at my choked cough. "Too much? Too corny? Yeah, I suppose it is." He drew us to a stop looking several shades of embarrassed, although he didn't look away. Instead, he met my stare. "I just want you to know I'm here with you wherever the journey takes us." He came up on his tiptoes and pressed a light kiss to my lips. "I will not run, Conall. Will you?"

I was stopped from answering when River called out, "Come on, stop with the mushy stuff. Calli wants to try boatin'."

Kyle laughed, though his eyes suggested we'd be revisiting this conversation. That was fine. By then, I hoped to have an answer to what I would do because the fear wanted to take charge when I wasn't sure if Kyle would wait for a criminal.

Mason came alongside, tugging Linc along with him. Linc was frowning, and I got the impression he'd overheard the conversation. Was he not happy for club members to date?

With no answer, I let myself be pulled along as River continued to encourage all of us to move quicker.

Stillhouse Lake was a hive of activity and made me wonder if it was like this every weekend. The bright day was warm. As I inhaled and listened, it was the scent and sounds of family. The place was beautiful. For all the activities going on, there was a relaxed, happy vibe.

Belton had a hidden gem, for sure.

Calli looked around as Linc explained why Mason was headed in a different direction. The marina sat opposite the boat slips River was leading us to.

Plonking down the basket of food, Kyle sat next to me on the wooden bench to wait.

"Have you been on a boat before?" Kyle asked, his thumb back to stroking my fingers.

"Nope." I glanced sideways at him. "You?"

The sun hit the top of his head, and his hair appeared to hold threads of spun gold. He'd put on a raggedy pair of denim shorts, similar to Linc's, that hugged his ass and showed how pert it was. He looked like a surfer dude, all windswept and tanned.

I'd barely spent time in the sun, and my legs were white compared to Kyle's. Not that he seemed to care, judging by the wolf whistle he'd given me when I'd come out of the bathroom wearing my cargo shorts that hadn't seen the light of day in years.

"A few times. It's fun when the breeze picks up and makes the boat fly over the waves."

My stomach dipped at the idea, and I eyed the water with concern.

"Breath slowly and focus on the horizon if you feel sick. That's what Mason told Poppy to do when he couldn't find his sea legs," River piped up. She lifted a leg and waggled it in the air. "Daddy says I got good sea legs."

"Thanks, Spirit. I thought you were told not to mention that?" Linc's long hair shifted over his shoulders as he reached out and plucked River up and tickled her sides, making her giggle.

The first time I'd heard him call River Spirit, I'd asked Nutty about it. She'd said it was because of his sister and that when she'd died, her spirit lived on in River. I'd seen the pictures in River's room of her mom, and they were alike. I could see the resemblance in Linc too.

Between bouts of giggles, she said, "Poppy, it's nothin' to be ashamed of."

Kyle leaned into my side and whispered, "I'm not sure Linc sees it that way."

Linc glanced at us, and the hard stare stopped Kyle from saying more, though it didn't remove the cheeky smile from his lips.

"There he is," Calli called as she started off toward the concrete boat ramp where a white, glossy sailboat, bigger than I'd thought, glided in under Mason's capable hands.

Stomach back to flipping, I unintentionally gripped Kyle's hand hard as we stood to follow the others after I'd picked up the basket. "You'll love it. It's like riding your motorcycle without a helmet. The wind blowing through your hair. Gives a genuine sense of freedom."

I muttered under my breath, "I fucking hope so," as I released Kyle's hand to give Mason the basket once Calli and River were safely aboard.

On board, the deck under my feet moved, but not enough to make me queasy. The lack of a strong wind helped, or so I thought, as the boat glided easily over the water at Mason's careful handling. We all had life jackets on, a safety precaution Mason insisted on. Not that I'd have argued when I was sure I wouldn't enjoy being toppled into the middle of the lake and require help for being foolish.

Laughter, the sound of the water lapping at the boat, and the dull throb of the engine somehow made it easy to relax on the padded seat. I lifted my face up and closed my eyes. The feel of the soft, warm breeze against my skin was nice. As was the feel of Kyle squeezed onto the seat next to me. We'd been sitting like that for a while.

The girls' giggles and chatter drifted from the far side of the boat.

My eyes slit open, and I watched Calli's head tip back as she laughed loudly at whatever River had said. The horrific situation that had brought us to Belton and caused her unknown trauma was unchangeable. But fuck, look what it had given her.

It was there for all to see. A life that she'd never have had in Round Rock. *And you...*a voice whispered.

My breath caught in my chest. Had my luck changed because of Calli's trauma? I hated the idea of it. Yet, here I was.

My first week at work was complete, and I hadn't fucked anything up. I made Sid smile. Something Ram said was a rarity except for Toad. The office was now a place where any person could lay their hands on what they needed. I wasn't sure what it said about me that I had an affinity for it and got a kick out of making things easier for Sid and the guys in the auto shop when they needed to know if we had parts and shit.

"Is everyone ready for the picnic?" Mason's question pulled me from my thoughts. He left the wheel when Linc did something with the anchor after calls of "yes" from everyone.

"I'm starvin'." Calli grinned at me. Face flushed from the sun, she looked like a poster ad for a carefree teenager.

The ugly reminder on my phone burned my gut at the possibility of this new life getting taken from her. I didn't care about myself. *Really?* Painful knots formed in my stomach at the truth of what I'd lose too.

Was it all gonna blow up in our faces?

I glanced at Kyle when he nudged me gently. Concern marred his brow. "Wanna eat?" he asked when I didn't move with everyone else to the table Mason placed the food on.

"Yeah, why not? Let's see if my sea legs work with my belly," I joked, aiming to keep my worry to myself because I wasn't sure how many more days I'd get if...

Leave it be. Give yourself this memory.

Chapter Twenty-Four

Kyle

I'd left Con asleep in bed. He'd slept for shit, tossing and turning for most of the night. It had been the same since Sunday, but last night was noticeably worse. At first, I'd considered maybe it was my confession, but he'd remained as veracious in the bedroom. Last night had been epic. Fuck, I'd have thought he was trying to memorize every part of me. If it wasn't me playing on his mind, then I suspected it had something to do with the situation in Round Rock. Something way more disturbing.

Had the cops reached out to him? To Mason? Had Earl woken up and spilled his guts? If that were the case, wouldn't they have arrested Con already?

Heaving a heavy sigh, I scowled at how each question brought several more. Calli was as concerned as me. She'd been casting me worried looks through the week as Con aimed for forced cheerfulness. Something he wasn't good at and made his behavior even more telling. Withdrawn behavior I could fathom and deal with. What we were getting wasn't Con's normal. Or not the man I'd come to know.

Huffing a breath, I glanced about the kitchen, looking for the fruit I'd laid down to finish packing the lunches. Putting the remaining items in the paper sacks, I lined them up on the counter. Glad everything was ready for them, I grabbed my bag and slung it over my back, leaving the apartment holding my helmet. It was my habit to make meals for Con and Calli, and they cleaned up. It worked, we were becoming a team, and I loved it. Calli and Con were a tight unit, and I wanted to be included. I wanted both of them in my life, in my home. We were nearly a month in, and it was working as far as I could tell.

Was I wrong? Was it too domesticated for Con? Was that what was on his mind?

On my hog, no closer to any answer, I was at work within minutes and far too quick to give my head some damn peace. The traffic was light as usual at that time of the morning. Parked in the place Linc allocated for staff, I ambled up the path to the house, helmet dangling from my fingers. I let myself into the shop and turned off the alarms, switching on lights as I headed toward the stairs. I made enough noise to alert Mason and Linc to the fact I was there.

Only once had I caught them naked, doing things I didn't want to think about when it came to Linc or Mason. No, seeing your boss getting nailed in spectacular style over the kitchen table by his suit-wearing boyfriend is not good for the heart. I'd had to creep back out to not alert them to my presence. And acted afterward like I'd seen nothing, when I'd admit, the way Mason handled Linc had aroused me the tiniest bit, dressed as he was in his suit and with Linc naked. It gave me a few ideas of what I'd like to do to Con if I got the chance.

Linc's head appeared over the stair railing, and I blushed at finding myself standing there thinking about Con naked and me fucking him on my kitchen table.

His dark brows merged as he frowned. "Another early appointment?" Before I could respond, he continued. "You gotta stop being so damn accommodating."

I chuckled, as it was his business he was telling me off for supporting. "Nah, I want a word with Mason if he's about."

The frown deepened before his head disappeared and the sound of boots hitting wood followed. I sighed and waited on the second floor.

"What's goin' on?" he asked as soon as he appeared.

There was no point beating around the bush, not when it came to Linc. "Con's acting odd, and I thought maybe it's got something to do with Earl, and I wanted to check in with Mason."

"Have you asked Con?"

I groaned and banged my helmet off my thigh. "Yes, all I get is 'I'm good' when clearly he's not. He's sleepin' for shit. Something is clearly on his mind, and I wanna help." I left out the way he'd been in bed the night before and the feelings it left me with. They were too personal.

Linc folded his arms over his chest and leaned his hips against the wooden rail. The look he wore warned me I wasn't gonna like what he had to say. "Maybe he doesn't want your help."

"That might be so. Then he needs to tell me that!" I snapped, then gave an apologetic smile to Linc when his eyes narrowed. "Sorry."

There was a sound from above, then shoes hit the wooden stairs.

Linc scowled as Mason appeared, looking ready to start his day in a crisp white shirt and black suit. "Hey, Kyle. You're here early."

"I wanted to ask if you know what's goin' on with Con?" I blurted out, ignoring the warning light in Linc's eyes.

An element of rigidity came and went that if I hadn't been looking at Mason to avoid Linc's glare, I'd have missed it. "You know what's wrong, don't you?"

"I'm sorry, but lawyer-client privilege means if you want answers, you need to speak to Conall."

"I fucking knew it!" I spun around and stomped into my room, anger and hurt driving me to throw my helmet harder on the counter than was sensible. It crashed into a tray holding tubs of packaged needles that tipped and spilled.

"He isn't hiding from you," Mason said from behind me.

Spinning back around, I found Mason alone, which surprised me with how I'd shouted at him in front of Linc. "Isn't he? He's clearly dealing with a problem, one he is *hiding* from me."

"What did I say to you last week? Con is like Linc. He deals with his crap *alone* because life has taught them both that the only people they can truly rely on, is themselves. Con trusts you." Mason held up his hand to stop me from denying it. "He does. He just doesn't know how to accept something given without strings. Without there having to be some form of payback. You should understand this better than anyone due to being a member of Dark Angels. They give nothing in this type of world. It's earned."

He came over to me and took hold of my shoulders. "You are the best thing that has probably ever happened to that man. Think about that." He let go and left me with my thoughts.

Half expecting Linc to come and kick my ass when he showed up four hours later after my client left, I rushed to apologize. "I shouldn't have yelled at Mason. I'm sorry."

Linc came and sat on my tattoo chair, his gaze now level with mine. "I heard what he said...about me." He shifted, not looking in the least bit comfortable as I kept quiet. "It's one of the hardest things to ask for help when raised how I suspect Con was. You learn it's a sign of weakness, one you don't want to show when others will use it against you. All you want in life is to prove you're worthy of respect...love." He got up and paced the room. "I fuckin' hate interferin' in folks' lives. That's Mason's job."

He swung and faced me. Anger was there, frustration, and also something he only shared with River and Mason, compassion. "Con and Mason are heading to Round Rock this afternoon. The cops want to talk to him in person."

My heart rate skyrocketed, and my hand clenched at my sides to stop them from shaking. The hurt cut deep, and I didn't know how to get my tongue to work with how heavy it felt in my mouth.

"I..." I sank onto the chair Linc had vacated moments before and stared dejectedly at him. The time we'd spent together had it meant nothing? I'd thought we were building trust, a relationship. Had I been wrong? "Fuck it to all hell! I only want to be there for him. Be his fucking person."

Linc ran his hands through his hair. "See, this is why I fucking hate this shit. Get the fuck up and get going. I'll have Nutty cancel the rest of your appointments and reschedule them. You'll have to work late for a few days to catch up."

Motionless, I stared at him, open-mouthed.

He shrugged, his cheeks going pink. "Get out of here if you don't want to miss him."

His words penetrated past the shock of what he was doing for me, and I bounced up. "Where are they leavin' from?"

"The auto shop."

I darted for the door as he shouted after me, "Don't you let on that I said a fuckin' word, or I'll kick your ass hard enough that you won't be able to sit for a month." The threat sounded real.

Halfway down the stairs, I cursed and headed back up to retrieve my helmet. Linc was there in the doorway, holding it.

"Thanks." I grabbed it and ran back down and out the front door, barely acknowledging Nutty as I flew past her.

In turmoil, I worked through valid reasons why I'd be visiting the auto shop, discarding each one when none sounded right in my head. By the time I pulled up outside the shop, I sort of had a plan in my head. At the absence of Mason's car, I dropped my helmet on my motorcycle and headed inside. I came to an abrupt stop at the sight of Sid. His brows arched, and he glanced toward the office where Con should be, then back at me.

"What you doin' here?" The mask of indifference was firmly in place and gave little away.

"I unexpectedly got the afternoon off and thought I'd see what time Con could skip out since it's Friday."

Sid's bald head glistened under the lights as he walked toward me, rubbing his greasy hands on a rag he took from the back of his overalls. "That so." He sniffed. "I smell bullshit."

He eyed me in a way that made me cave faster than a rock slide. "Listen, Linc will kick my ass if Con figures out I'm here because I know he's off to Round Rock." I sagged when the engine in the background cut off, and my voice carried. Shit, could Con hear from the office what was happening in the workshop?

The nod from Sid drew my attention. My eyes narrowed when it became apparent that Sid knew Con's situation. I glanced around, assessing if anyone else knew what was going on. The lack of attention eased a little of the tension inside me.

As I glanced back at Sid, he muttered, "Then you're gonna need to learn to lie better."

Chapter Twenty-Five

Conall

There was little point sighing when I heard Kyle when the sound of an engine reeving cut out. I got up and peered out the door. Kyle's expression hid none of the hurt when he met my gaze. Fuck, who'd told him?

I'd kept my stress about the visit Mason had planned to Round Rock to myself. Several times I'd been tempted to speak up about what would happen today. But I couldn't bring myself to do it and remove his happiness. To bring into reality that I might lose what we had.

So I'd kept quiet and hoped that I wouldn't regret it. That was still in the balance judging by Kyle's stance. The Round Rock Police Department had been vague about the need to speak to me. Was there any point in causing Kyle and Calli undue stress?

A pitiful excuse to justify my actions, and right now, that was cold comfort. The man who'd offered me unconditional help and more looked like he didn't know me as he walked stiffly toward me.

"You know, don't you?" It wasn't really a question, but he nodded. It didn't seem relevant how he'd found out, only that it had hurt him. Something I could see I'd done even when it was what I'd wanted to avoid. How the fuck did I fix this?

I stepped back to let him pass. If he was going to dump my ass, I didn't want an audience. I shut the door on Sid's scowling face and then turned to face Kyle. "I'm sorry for keeping..." I started, then stopped when he came and got in my face.

His neck strained back so he could look me in the eye. God, he was beautiful. "Am I the only one invested in making what this is between us work?"

The despair in his voice made me slide my hands around his middle to hold him. "No, you aren't the only one invested in this. I...you..." I buried my face in his hair, inhaling his scent, needing a moment to absorb how fucking lucky I was.

Last night I'd tried to show him in every way I knew how much he meant to me. I'd wanted those memories if everything went to shit today. "I don't wanna lose what we've got. I don't."

A shuddery breath caught in my throat at the truth. "This past week, knowing that I could lose you, lose Calli. Fuck, it hurt. Hurt like nothing ever has. Not even my Ma dying made me feel like this." I wanted him to understand, so I did something I'd never done and confessed my fear aloud.

"I'm...scared, Ky...scared of losing everything." Taking another shuddery breath, I lifted my head, needing to see him.

His glittering gaze gouged my heart. "Don't shut me out, Con. Let me be there to share the burden. I'm not going anywhere. I swear, whatever happens today, I'm gonna be there for you. For Calli. I'll wait for you." The depth of emotion was impossible to miss.

I sniffed, blinking at the ache at the back of my eyes. Was it possible? How could he say those things with such conviction? I searched his gaze, seeing nothing but the truth I'd heard in his words.

What had I done to deserve this man? "Okay." I pressed my forehead to his, holding his gaze. "I'm sorry I fucked up." I put as much sincerity as possible into the words.

"Good, 'cause when we get back tonight, your ass is mine, and I'm gonna remind you..."—he came up and kissed my lip—"repeatedly how to use your words."

A delicious shiver ran through me and lodged itself in my balls. The smile he wore made me swallow hard. "I can live with that." I kissed him hard, needing reassurance that we were okay and holding on to the hope he'd get to deliver on his promise.

The door opening at my back brought me back to my senses.

"Well, it would seem we have an extra passenger for the trip." The sarcastic edge to Mason's voice didn't go unnoticed when Kyle winced as he stepped back.

"Con invited me," Kyle muttered, not quite looking Mason in the eye.

"As a lawyer, you learn to read people easily, Kyle! Linc..." Mason shook his head and looked at me. "You ready?"

I reached for Kyle's hand and interlaced our fingers. "Yeah."

The trip hadn't taken too long, and we'd all remained silent for most of it. It was difficult to talk sensibly with how much was running through my head. I was glad Kyle was with me. That didn't mean I wanted to spout all the crap going on inside my mind. My head had been working overtime since Mason and I had spoken on Monday about the message.

Today was the only time Mason had space to take the trip, one for a moment I'd considered taking alone. Mason had set me straight on that and suggested I talk to Kyle. With the fresh memory of Kyle's hurt expression, I wish I'd listened.

The sight of the police station had Kyle leaning forward in the back seat to place a hand on my shoulder. The pressure was reassuring, even if it did nothing to calm the storm inside me.

Engine switched off, Mason shifted to look at me. "Just a reminder. I'll do the talking unless I indicate otherwise. Got it?"

"Yup."

Dressed in a T-shirt with the auto shop logo that Mason insisted I leave on, I got out of the car and waited for Kyle. The three of us walked toward the flat roof, single-story building with blue bars in front of the windows. I'd been fortunate enough never to have stepped foot inside the place.

Noise and the scent of terrible coffee were my first impressions. Then came the narrowed-eyed stares of those in the reception area. Mason walked up with an air of authority I attempted to replicate. Only a minute later, we were all ushered into a room painted off-white. A scratched table and four chairs sat in the room with no windows. The flooring looked to have taken a beating, though it was clean.

My skin itched, and the impulse to open the door to get some fresher air was hard to resist. Before it could become an actual issue, the door opened, revealing a large, dark-haired man wearing a standard police uniform carrying a file.

He nodded at Mason while ignoring Kyle and me. Mason had informed the front desk who Kyle was and that he was there to support me.

"Sit," he demanded, not doing any introductions. He moved the one remaining seat so he wasn't sitting next to Mason but facing him.

Kyle's brows raised as he looked at me. I shrugged, unsure if this was some tactic. Ignore the suspect and act like an asshole.

"Officer Franklin, we are here." The smile was all hard edges, as was the glint in Mason's eyes. "Now, can you explain what required my client to be here in person? As I stated on the phone, my client is a busy man. We've been more than accommodating to your department and supplied everything you've asked for." Mason's tone was abrupt in a way I'd never heard before.

Franklin opened the file and held it so no one could see what was inside. The air in the room became harder to inhale. "There are some concerns regarding timelines that need clearing up and some clarity about some actions *your client* has taken since the attack. There is also some evidence that requires some explainin'. I'm sure you and *your client* wish to cooperate and clear up these matters."

If Franklin's disdain was to get a reaction, he got nothing, although my gut was getting a workout.

"My client has already given a timeline on his and his sister's whereabouts at the time of the assault. I sent the email after we'd gone through it with you." The reply came in a whiplash tone.

Franklin shifted in his seat, his eyes narrowing on Mason, who didn't seem in the least bit concerned at the anger aimed at him by the other man. "That might be the case. DNA evidence suggests that both your client and his sister were present in the trailer at the time of the attack." His beady eyes gleamed with malice as he shifted his stare to me.

It was impossible to breathe. Years of practice held me still in the chair as I figured out what they possibly meant.

"What evidence? My client's and his sister's DNA would be all over the trailer. Mr. Levitt lived with Mr. Regan and his sister and shared communal spaces. So it comes to reason he'd have their DNA on his skin."

Franklin sat forward, his jaw jutting out. "That might be the case. It would definitely not account for it being all over the victim. Particularly his penis." The last was spat in my direction.

The room spun, and suddenly it wasn't only me who felt at risk. My lips parted, and Mason's eyes connected with mine, issuing a warning I heeded... for now, as long as Calliope remained out of this.

Mason crossed his legs, looking fully relaxed. "Just to clarify, are you advising that a sample of Ms. Regan's DNA was on Mr. Levitt's penis?"

At the nod, Mason continued, "From my recollection of the attack on Mr. Levitt and the evidence you supplied to my office, the bloody condition of Mr. Levitt and the state of the trailer means cross-contamination clearly cannot be ruled out. Are you suggesting otherwise? Because this appears to be a fishing expedition at my client's expense."

Franklin's face darkened as he gave a noncommittal head movement that did little to ease the tension radiating up my back.

"Then shall we move on to the timeline issue?" Mason continued and ran through what we'd said previously without missing a beat. We'd stuck close to the truth in case I'd been seen the night of the attack. Listening to him now, I understood why he was so good at his job.

Franklin leveled me with an aggressive stare when Mason finished speaking. "You should know that Mr. Levitt regained consciousness several days ago and is recovering well, with no signs of memory problems. It'll only be a matter of time before we find out the truth about who attacked him."

My blood ran cold. "Why are you selling the trailer?" he continued, switching topics so fast it took a second to register what he asked.

I caught Mason's tightening jaw before he tugged on the cuff of his shirt. I shrugged. "Why would I keep it? It's mine and Calli's legally." Another shrug as I stared the officer directly in the eye. "We got no reason to stay here. It's no secret that Earl and I didn't get along. So there's nothing to keep me here."

He sneered. "Not even your so-called brothers."

"We need the money to get a deposit on an apartment in Belton. I can't keep relying on folks good will forever, can I?" I replied, ignoring his barb about Chosen Few.

Franklin's snort showed his disbelief, but Mason's lips lifted at the edges at my answer. "Is there anything else, Officer Franklin?"

He shook his head, looking pissed off as he scowled and closed the file.

Somehow, minutes later, I was free and standing next to Mason's car. He motioned for us to get in wordlessly. Doors shut, he glanced in my direction. "We need to go and see Dog now and find out if anyone has been to warn Earl to keep his mouth shut."

Chapter Twenty-Six

Kyle

I'd nearly shit my pants when the asshole had brought up the DNA and where they'd found it. The terror for Calli had taken every ounce of willpower to keep seated and act like the officer hadn't hammered a nail into me. I'd remained quiet in the car as Mason reassured Con that if they'd had anything more, they'd have arrested him. Mason suggested bringing Con to Round Rock was an attempt at goading a reaction out of him over the DNA evidence to see if he'd incriminate himself to protect his sister. Did they think Calli had beaten Earl? I supposed they hadn't ruled out anything, especially with her brother being part of a chapter like Chosen Few.

"I suspect they've formed a picture of the events that happened. However, with nothing concrete and Calliope being a minor, they need you with her during questioning, so as I said, you were the easier target." Mason glanced sideways for a brief second. "You did good."

"Let's hope," Con muttered, sounding anything but hopeful.

Something that left me with a bitter taste in my mouth when it came to a future of no Con. When the clubhouse came into view, the number of motorcycles out front added to my disquiet for Con and what might happen next.

We'd barely gotten out of the car when Dog appeared in the doorway, his impenetrable gaze fixed on Con. "Go around the back, to the side door." He disappeared inside, and a stony-faced Con walked off to the left side of the one-story nondescript building that looked like a large brick trailer.

The weight of stares came from the windows I couldn't see through because they were coated in something that prevented folks from looking in.

I walked with Mason in the same direction as Con, hoping the brothers weren't planning anything. I would have Con's back, no matter the cost.

At a wooden door, Con reached for the handle, only for it to open. Rattlesnake grinned at us and pulled Con in for a hug. "Good to see ya, man." He nodded at me. "Kyle, been a while. How's it hangin'?"

"Rattlesnake, when you've finished checking how everyone is..." Dog's gruff voice came from inside.

Rattlesnake didn't cower, but he did straighten and step back to allow us to enter what appeared to be a small office. The desk Dog was sitting behind held several cell phones and nothing else. Shelves behind him held motorcycle parts. The only furniture was two seats in front of the desk and the chair Dog was sitting in.

Dog pointed to the chairs, and Con and Mason sat. I stood to the side, close enough to Con if he needed me, as I stared at Dog, daring him to make a move.

"I take it you heard Earl's awake?" Dog asked, getting straight to the point.

Mason nodded. "The police department wanted to speak to Con, and they kindly let us know. Is there a reason you didn't reach out?" His tone didn't suggest it was kind of them at all.

"I was letting the heat die down." His gaze shifted to Con. "I went and had a word with him. Let him know what'll happen if he opens his trap."

"Thanks," Con spat out.

A loud sigh followed. Dog leaned his enormous, leather-clad bulk on the table. "I get that you're pissed. Isn't me greasin' the way with Linc to get you into Dark Angels enough?"

Con glanced at Mason, who shrugged, looking as surprised by this news as I was. "Is that what you did?" Con asked when he looked back at Dog.

"I did. I fucked up the situation here, trying to keep everything tight so it would stop the cops from sniffing around after the business with…" He looked at Mason, and I understood that whatever the business was, it wasn't legal.

Dog looked back at Con, and I could see the regret. "I wanted to set it right. You were a solid brother and deserved better. My friendship with Earl…yeah, it fucked shit up. I couldn't see that he'd...do what you accused him of. I realize that shouldn't have come into it. I'll admit I'm still struggling with it all after he eventually confessed."

The man looked to age right before my eyes as he sagged in his seat, looking a little defeated. It wasn't an apology, but it was probably the closest Con would get.

"Why did you reach out to Killer without askin' if it was what I wanted?" Whatever Con felt about this situation, or Dog's struggle with Earl's behavior, there was nothing in his tone to give it away.

"Got the impression the last time we spoke that hearin' from me was not what you wanted." He nodded at Rattlesnake. "So I got someone else to keep in touch, suss out the situation, then I spoke to Killer. Made sure I fixed things for you."

This was news.

Mason looked between both men. "Can we go back to Earl because I don't think us being here too long is advisable." Dog's head bobbed. "Are you sure Earl won't say a word?"

The evil smile chilled me to my core. Killer was dangerous when riled. It seemed Dog was cut from the same cloth. "He won't say nothin', not if he wants to keep breathin'. You and Calli are safe. I swear as president of Chosen Few, he won't be botherin' you again."

Club justice could be brutal if a member betrayed his brothers, and from the look on Dog's face, I didn't doubt Dog would keep his word if Earl spilled his guts to the wrong person.

Con was safe... *hopefully!*

On the drive back, Con did most of the talking as if processing that Dog had done something for him and that, in the end, he'd had Con's back. We could only hope that Earl kept his mouth shut and the cops got nothing concrete on Con carrying out the attack.

"Is Calli staying at Linc's tonight?" I asked as we entered the apartment, my mind taking a detour at the flex of the denim-covered ass in front of me. I needed to release some of the tension from the week of stress, and my earlier promise was, to my mind, the best way to achieve it.

Con watched me shut the door as he kicked off his shoes. "Yup."

We'd stopped for pizza on the way home, so food wasn't at the top of anyone's agenda for the evening. He met my stare as I followed and toed off my sneakers. Keeping his gaze, I unbuckled my belt, sliding it free. The smile I aimed at him caused his eyelids to dip and his chest to heave.

I looped the leather through the buckle and walked to him. "Take off your shirt. I have a promise to fulfill."

His breathing became erratic when the shirt landed on the floor, and he eyed the belt. I reached out and slid his hand into the loop, then took the end and fed it back through the buckle, creating another loop to slip over his free wrist. I tugged the end of the leather, bringing him close enough for his body to touch mine. He wasn't trapped, but I wanted the illusion he was. That he was my captive. "You gonna let me make you mine?"

His breath hit my warm skin as he nodded. The sexual tension ramped up as I tugged again on the leather and led him to the table in the far corner of the room. The idea of taking him naked while still dressed was thanks to Mason and Linc.

Dropping the leather, I wrapped my hands around his leather-clad wrists, squeezing. "Stay here, and don't move."

A dark flush coated his cheeks, the desire hard to look away from. Sucking in a deep Con-scented breath, I moved to get a condom and lube from my bedroom. I was pleased to see he was exactly where I'd left him when I returned.

It was hard not to admire his chest covered in artwork. The way his muscles flexed as he offered a challenge I would never turn down. Until now, he'd always been the one to top, and I couldn't wait to make him fly for the first time.

I placed the lube and condom on the table, then helped him to remove his remaining clothes. The black leather dangling from his wrists was a huge fucking turn-on as it hung next to his semi-hard cock. When I reached for the leather belt, his gaze traveled down my clothed body.

"I'm gonna fuck you over the table." I came nearer and rose to get closer to his face. "Naked and with me dressed. I'm gonna make you learn a new way of finding those words you struggle with so you never forget them again." A shiver rippled through him, and his cock hardened further and pushed at my thigh.

"Is that so?" he rasped sexily, his eyes challenging me.

"Yes!" Leather in hand, I positioned him on the table and left his arms stretched out, the leather lying on the surface of the wood. "Don't move your arms," I whispered next to his ear before going to admire his ass.

Firm and round, I admired the tattoos that went over his left buttock and down his leg as I stroked the skin. My fingertips trailed over them, and I loved the tiny moan Con made. "So beautiful. One day, I hope you'll let me put my ink on you." I traced over his right hip. "Here"—I moved over the unmarked skin—"or maybe here."

He didn't answer, which was okay because I wanted to come up with the right piece of artwork for him, and that would take time. I didn't linger in any one place for long. Touching him, feeling him move and moan, built a sexy tension between us.

By the time I moved to bend and stroke my tongue over his twitching hole, he was repeatedly cursing, wanting me to quicken the pace.

"Let me learn what you like," I murmured against his hole at the next curse. I wanted to memorize every part of him and note what made him whimper, cry, and beg for more.

Sweat coated his skin as I deliberately worked my tongue into his ass. The muscle clenched on my tongue as his dark, musky flavor filled my senses.

"Fuck...oh fuck...yeah...fuck."

I jabbed in deeper as the muscle loosened. My hand stroked his balls, sliding them together in the sac as he rocked back, rubbing his cock against the table. The sound of metal hitting wood came and went with each move.

My cock hurt as it pressed against my fly, desperate to take the place of my tongue. But I wasn't finished. Fuck, I never wanted to stop tasting him.

When I reached over to where I'd left the lube and flicked open the lid, he was moaning and rocking continually. I released his balls to pour a liberal amount into my hand. Bottle on the table, I coated both hands, then returned to stroking his balls while I carefully slid a finger into his ass, then added my tongue. The whimper was long as my tongue became motionless while I slowly pushed the finger deeper into his slick channel.

A deep guttural groan came with his left leg lifting, his knee going onto the table, opening his ass to me. "More, I need more," he panted between gasps.

I couldn't see his face, but the desperation was clear to hear.

My reply was to work tongue and finger together, stretching him and giving him what he begged for. Feeling for his sweet spot, I gently rubbed over it, getting more sounds and his ass working to impale itself on my face.

The throbbing cock, crushed in my jeans, was getting harder to ignore when Con sang like a damn canary. Trembling with need, I pulled my tongue and finger free. I wiped my mouth with a shaking hand, my other going to the button on my jeans. Breath hissed through my teeth as my cock hit the air. Red and slick with need, my jaw clenched as I grabbed the condom and tore it open with my teeth. The coil of desire in the pit of my stomach buzzed with a life of its own as I sheathed myself fast enough to consider it a world record.

Reaching for the lube, the air in my chest caught in my throat as Con raised his head to look back over his shoulder. The hunger in his feverish gaze made my legs tremble and my cock throb with the need to spill my seed.

I picked up the lube and dumped it over the condom. It dripped over his ass and down his crack, making a mess in my haste. Bottle down, I worked some of it into his ass, then took hold of his hips, hoping he was ready for what I wanted to do. I was by no means small, but I was at the end of my patience.

His ass canted up, and the knee on the table slid higher. I groaned at the sight of him, my fingers digging into his flesh. Unable to hold back any longer, I pushed the head of my cock against the hot, slick rim and applied pressure.

Con whimpered. "Fuck, so big."

He cut off my chuckle when he canted back, and his ass swallowed the head of my cock. The muscles convulsed around me as I panted and willed my cock to not shoot its load at the pleasure-pain overload. It had been a long time since I'd fucked a guy, and that it was Con made me very trigger-happy.

"Fucker, move, goddamnit," he snarled, his lips peeling back as he gasped and panted. His body was shaking against the table.

I reached over him, my cock sinking deeper into the clasping channel, and took hold of the leather belt, wrapping it around my fist. I tugged it hard to bring his arms up off the table. Holding tight, with my other hand on his hip, I growled as his head thumped on the table.

"You asked for it." I slammed home. Flesh slapping against flesh drowned out my ragged breathing as I locked my knees to give him what he wanted.

Sensations bombarded me as Con mewled and begged for more, and the world became a myriad of color, sound, smell, and feelings. They all merged as I gave Con everything he demanded and my heart pounded against my ribs. My balls throbbed with the need to come inside the hot convulsing sheath, making me wish nothing separated us.

Sweat dripped down my forehead and the sides of my face, hair stuck to my skin as I powered into the man who I'd wanted from the first moment I'd seen him.

His whole body shuddered, and I let go of the belt, hand reaching under him to feel his cock pulsing cum over my table. I stroked his silky, hard length prolonging his orgasm. His cry was nothing more than a whisper when his ass clamped on my cock, squeezing it so tight my eyes crossed, milking the cum from me.

My movements became erratic as furious bursts of cum filled the condom. I collapsed over his back, wheezing while trying to regain my breath with the tiny aftershocks kicking up my cock, giving Con everything in my balls.

Glued together, I figured it had to be uncomfortable, but I had no energy to move. He'd taken it all. "I can't feel my legs," I muttered through dry lips.

"Try lying against this table and being squished into the wood," he slurred.

A chuckle rumbled up my chest, and my semi-hard cock shifted in his ass, getting a moan of complaint. "If you're lookin' to go again, I can tell you my ass ain't."

The rumble turned into full-blown laughter, and I eased up and back, taking hold of the base of the condom as I moved out of his body.

"I clearly heard you asking for more," I said through my exhausted laughter as I tied off the condom and dropped it on the floor so I could help Con up when he didn't move.

He wasn't in much better shape than I was. Cum covered the table and him as he slung his arm over my shoulder, the belt hanging from his wrist as he leaned on me.

I grunted. "Fuck, you're heavy."

"Then next time fuck me in bed where we don't have to move," he mumbled, his cheeks flushing darker.

"What would be the fun in that?" I grinned at him when he glanced sideways.

"Next time, you get to lie on the table."

I could live with that.

Epilogue

Kyle

Two Months Later

Aware that the three-month timeline I'd given Con was up, an idea had formed, something to show Con I wanted him to stay. I'd waited until he'd left for work that morning and Calli had gone to school. My Friday had been full, but I'd gotten a couple of cancellations that I used to my advantage. One was this morning, and the second was this afternoon. And that meant the design for Con's tattoo that I'd been tinkering with could get a bit more attention. If I wasn't at work, I was with Con and Calliope, meaning it limited me to doing it when no one was around to watch over my shoulder.

Inking him was something I'd become fixated on. Con was careful about what went on his body, and I really wanted to give him something special. A piece of artwork that represented who he was.

Before that, I had something else to do. Going into his old room, I eyed the space and grinned at how very few of Con's things were in the room. My smile widened when I reached the closet and found it empty. I went to the tall boy at the end of the bed against the wall and opened the top drawer. There was little in there aside from a couple of old T-shirts. I gathered what there was in my arms and opened the second drawer, grabbing underwear. I carried it into our room and laid it in the empty drawers I'd cleared minutes earlier.

Back in the room for a second trip, I emptied the next two drawers, doing the same thing. When I got to the last drawer, my heart skittered to a stop at the battered tin sitting on its own. It looked forlorn, battered, and dented. The paint was peeling, leaving rust spots. It looked very sorry for itself. My fingers were shaking as I reached out, feeling all kinds of things that were hard to put into words. Was this what he'd dug out of the mess at the back of the trailer? At the time, I'd thought it odd and worried about the reason behind hiding it. Then it slipped my mind.

Expecting it to be heavier, the lack of weight surprised me. In my hand, I eyed the tin. It was wrong on so many levels to pry. I knew it. Yet something pushed me. Knowing Con, I didn't consider it to be something bad. More that it might reveal a little more about him and his past, one he didn't share often. Before I could overthink it or stop myself, I flicked the lid open. It creaked, and my lips trembled at the contents.

A lump lodged in the back of my throat, and my nose burned as I reached into it and picked out the small bracelet with Calliope's name. The love for his sister was never more evident than in the small bit of plastic bracelet the maternity staff must have put around her ankle after her birth. That Con had kept it showed a real sentimental side that I bet no one ever got to see. At that moment, an idea formed, and I rushed out of the bedroom, the tin clutched in my hand.

At work, I pulled out the tin I'd hidden in the bag I used to carry my shit when riding my motorcycle. I had no memory of the ride to work as I ran through all the items in the tin and how I could make them all fit my design. Excitement poured through me as I shut my door, then laid out the items in the tin. Going to the drawer that held my pencils, inks, and paper for drawing, I took out the sheet for Con.

I'd put it at the bottom of the pile in case anyone went searching. It wasn't that it embarrassed me. It was more that I wanted Con to see it first when it was done. I sat at my workbench and glanced between the items and what I'd already done. Pencil in hand, I worked to adapt what I'd already created.

So lost in what I was doing, I blinked at the noise behind me. I shifted to cover the bench at the next knock on my door.

"Your first client is here," Nutty called through the closed door.

Breath hissed through my teeth as I cursed. "Gimme two," I called back.

A sigh escaped as I quickly put everything away, resigned for now at putting the sketch to one side to work on that afternoon. "Later, you can do more later." One last look at what I'd done, and my smile returned. Fuck, it was some of my best work!

• • • ● ● • ● • • •

C onall

Sitting at the office desk, I answered the ringing phone, "Stone's auto shop, how can I help?" Sid had decided two months earlier, at my prompting, to transfer all calls to one phone so I could take over the booking system, which before was scraps of paper someone wrote on when they took a call. Then they'd eventually move it onto the work schedule.

"Con, it's Mason."

My heart sped up. "Hey, everything okay?" I'd been waiting on the money coming through for the sale of the trailer. The piece of shit had sold for sixty-thousand dollars, more than I would've ever paid for it.

Rattlesnake and two other brothers had cleaned it up to make it look presentable. They must have done a good job to get me that kind of money. It was another peace offering from Dog. Earl was now in a rehab place somewhere, or so I'd been told. Not that I cared. As long as he kept his mouth shut, then he could rot in hell for me. From what I'd gleaned, the case was no longer active, or some such thing was how Mason explained it to me. I didn't care as long as they didn't come after Calli or me.

We were both happy with the new life we had. To that end, I pushed the niggle about Earl to the back of my mind. Most of the time, it worked. Running from the shit had brought me a new life. And it had brought Calli a life where she could be a normal teenager. The therapy was going okay, or so she said, and I believed her when she said she was making new friends.

"Yes, everything is fine. I'm calling to let you know the money came through for the trailer, and I've had it transferred into the joint account you have with Calli, as agreed."

"We never talked about how much I owe you for all...this." By my calculation, we were close to ninety thousand in the account. So far, we'd touched none of it.

"Beer and popcorn."

"Huh?"

"The toffee-coated kind. That will more than pay your bill."

I eyed the phone before putting it back to my ear, convinced I'd heard wrong. "You ain't serious?"

"As a heartbeat. Beer and popcorn, that's my price."

"Erm..." I scratched my jaw. "I can run with that," I half-joked, trying to tell myself he was a brother who just wore a suit. I was getting better at the accepting thing... some days.

"Great. Are you comin' Sunday to the family barbeque with Calli?"

I blinked at the switch in conversation. "Ky mentioned it. Isn't that a family thing?"

When Kyle had talked about it, I was sure it was Mason's family going to Linc's home, not the brothers from Dark Angels. Why would he be inviting us?

"You doofus, you and Calli are family. Ask River." He chuckled. "Anyway, it starts at two, and don't forget my beer and popcorn. See ya." A second later, the phone went silent.

I shook my head and placed my phone down. How could I argue with folks that didn't give me a chance to answer? Kyle was the same. I couldn't help but grin at how fucking happy that made me when it came to him. I'd learned that though Kyle aimed for laid-back, he could have an iron will when getting what he wanted.

"You planning on knocking off or sitting there grinning like a fool?" Toad asked as he came into the office with a bunch of papers in his hand.

Another thing that had changed in the auto shop was invoices. The guys knew I'd kick their asses if they didn't come to me as soon as they arrived so I could ensure they got logged and stuff didn't get missed.

"I'll take those." Checking the time before reaching out, my eyes widened. "Where the fuck did the day go?" On Fridays, we all finished at three-thirty, and it was a little after that.

"In spray paints."

"Did you finish Matt's paint job?" I'd checked out the cost of one of Toad's hand-painted tanks, and as much as I'd love one, there was no way I'd waste money on it, not when I needed to have a conversation with Kyle about the three-month deadline we'd set. There were no money issues now, and I could more than afford an apartment with Calli. The very thought of leaving twisted me up in knots.

"I did. It's the fucking bomb." Toad perched his ass on the arm of the seat and folded his arms. "You got a look that says you got somethin' on your mind. Wanna share?"

We'd become friends and occasionally met outside work to shoot the breeze and talk shit. "The money came through for the trailer."

Toad frowned. "That's good news, ain't it?"

"It is...it's just I could move out of Ky's now."

He got a knowing look I'd seen a time or two before as he asked bluntly, "Do you wanna?"

That was easy to answer. "No."

His grin widened. "Then what's the issue? 'Cause right now, I ain't seeing one."

"When we originally moved in with Ky, we decided on a three-month trial."

"Yeah, and?"

His expression clearly showed he didn't get my issue. "It's up. What if he wants me to move out?"

The belly laugh was so unexpected that I stared at Toad as he rocked, holding his middle. "Why you laughin' like that?"

"You, you're a funny fucking dude. Kyle would kick himself out before he ask you to leave. The man is fucking starry-eyed over you." Toad reached over the organized desk and picked up the nearly empty lunch sack Kyle had prepared for me. "He makes you a lunch bag," he said through laughter. "He's too fucking cute for words. I've seen the treats he puts in there."

"Hey." I scowled, finding it hard not to see the funny side when Toad put it like that. Kyle was cute with his lunch sack prep. "Okay, he likes me..."

"Like, such a damn insipid word. But whatever, man." Toad got up. "You need to get your butt out of that chair and go and speak to him, and you'll see I'm right."

He left, and I stared at the open door, only then noticing the quiet. The noise hardly registered anymore. It was just background sound when I noticed it.

Out of my chair, I sorted the invoices into the to-be-paid box and checked that I'd shut everything down before grabbing my jacket and keys. Moving with purpose, I tried to recall what Kyle had mentioned he had going on today.

No closer to figuring it out when I pulled into Linc's driveway, I got off my hog, leaving my helmet on the seat. There were a few other vehicles about, which suggested the shop was busy. I didn't sigh at having to wait, but it was a close call. My man was popular. He'd not mentioned inking me since the first time, and I hadn't figured out a way to bring it up again. I wanted his ink on me. Wanted his mark. It was a first for me, and I was still figuring that out.

Walking through the door, my gaze swept the reception area, noting the three guys waiting.

Nutty gave me a sunny smile as she answered the phone tucked to her ear, "Yes, Kyle has a space on July tenth. Do you want me to pencil you in?" She nodded toward the stairs and mouth, "He's free. Go on up."

I gave her a wave and went up the stairs. Kyle's door was partially open, and music poured out that I was clueless to identify. He really liked some weird shit! I tapped on the doorframe as I poked my head inside, pushing the door wide.

The music was so loud he didn't so much as glance up. His back was to me, and his foot tapped as he focused on what was in front of him. When he was designing artwork, he could shut everything else out.

But it wasn't him that pulled me deeper into the room. It was the battered, old tin sitting next to him. He glanced at it and then back to what he was doing. My tin, the one I'd put in the bottom drawer of the dresser in the bedroom that I hadn't slept in for months.

What the fuck was he doing with it? Had he been snooping on me?

I tapped him on the shoulder hard enough to get him to jerk and twist toward me. A guilty look appeared as his gaze darted to the tin and back to me.

"Wanna explain?" I asked loud enough to be heard over the music. Feelings I wasn't sure how to deal with stung like bees.

Kyle got up and went to where he'd laid his phone next to a speaker and messed with the screen before the music switched off, leaving silence. Tension rolled off the man, who wasn't quite meeting my gaze as he scuffed his sneaker on the floor in front of him.

The silence lengthened, and my gaze went back to the tin. It held all my treasures, all the little things that held value to me. A ticket stub from my first concert, a little batman car I'd begged for at a fair that we probably hadn't been able to afford, but Mom had gotten it for me anyway. The bracelet a baby gets when they're in the hospital, which was Calli's. There were more things like that. Nothing was worth anything other than the memory of how they'd made me feel. They were personal to me and no one else, and I wasn't sure how I felt about him seeing this part of me.

Why would he take them?

It was then I caught sight of the drawing on the counter. A sting at the backs of my eyes had me blinking away the unwanted sudden rush of tears. I swallowed and took a shaky breath as I moved closer and stared at the design clearly meant for me.

In the artwork were my mementos laid on a rucked blanket, ready to scoop them up and keep them safe. And there in the middle was Calliope. What I treasured most. The likeness was uncanny, and I could already imagine it on my skin.

"I found the box when I shifted all your things into my room. I promise I wasn't snooping. Then...fuck, I did snoop, and I know it's wrong, but when I saw what was inside, I got this wild idea, and...oh fuck, I'm sorry. Please don't be mad at me. I'd been working on this idea, then I saw the tin, and well..."

I slowly turned to face him. Face the person who would look to take all my happy memories from a crappy childhood and turn them into something beautiful, into art. The thickness in my throat made it hard to speak. "It's beautiful, thank you."

"You like it? Really?" He came toward me, looking uncertain.

I pulled him into my arms and kissed him with all the emotions that made him my special person on a different level from Calli. Not better, just different. "I'm staying. The trial is over," I murmured against his mouth.

He chuckled against my lips, making them vibrate. "What trial? I don't know what you're talking about." His fingers ran down my sides, and then they dug in, holding on as he deepened the kiss.

When we broke, gasping for air, I was horny as fuck. The hand he slid over my right hip in a propriety way didn't help. "Wanna see how we can make the design fit?"

"How much is this gonna cost me?"

The smile brightened the entire room, right along with my heart. "I'm sure we can work that out on the kitchen table when we get home..." He winked sexily, causing my cock to buck. "Isn't Calli staying at her friend's tonight?"

She'd made friends with Mina's oldest daughter, whose sister was Luna, River's best friend. "I believe so."

"Then you're in luck. You can make a down payment today."
He moved until I pressed as close to him as two people could
get. "Then we can come up with a long-term payment plan.
You know, the kind that might take a very, very, long time to
pay off."

I nodded, eyes hooding as his mouth tempted me. "I think I
can work with those terms." The latter I murmured against his
lips as they parted, and I got lost in the man who'd made running from my darkness the right decision because it matched
his light to perfection. I wasn't running anymore. I was home.

Other Books by the Author

Standalone

When Fake Changed Everything
Christmas beyond Christmas
The Elves and the Bondage Daddy (Grim and Sinister
Delights Book 5)
Agrippa My Heart
His Boy to Tease
Headshot
A Brat For Kinkmas

Series

Tangled Tentacles Series
Alexi #1

Victor #2
Todd #3
Markov # 4

Little Paws Haven Series
Little Treasure he Hides

The Potters Creek Series
A Christmas Wish (book one)

The App Series
The App: Daddy kink (book one)
The App: Littles (book two)
The App: Puppy play (book three)
The Flamingo Bar Series
Always More (book one)
The Little Side of Me (book two)
3 Is the Magic Number (book three)

La Trattoria Di Amore Series
Puzzle Pieces (book one)
Dominated but not Subdued (book two)
Made to Submit

The Playroom Series
Mine, Body and Soul: Part One

Mine, Body and Soul: Part Two

Mine, Body and Soul: Part Three

Ferron's Journey: Damaged Part One (book four)

Ferron's Journey: Hidden Part Two (book five)

Ferron's Journey: Revelation Part Three (book six)

Mine, Body and Soul Trilogy

Ferron's Journey Trilogy

Spinoff Love's Heart Print

Dark River Stone Collective Series

The Light Beneath the Dark (Book One)

When Darkness Turns to Light (Book Two)

The Billionaire Playground Series

Property of a Billionaire (Book one)

Reluctant Billionaire (Book two)

Billionaire's Muse (Book three)

Heart Stones Series

Blood King

The Manx Cat Guardians Series Where it all Began: Origins
(Book 1)

Seeing Beyond the Scars (Book 2)

Destiny Collides Past and Present (Book 3)

Searching for a Soul to Love (Book 4)

The 12 Disasters of Christmas (Book 5)

Laws of Attraction (Book 6)

The Teacher's Boy (Book 7)

Boxset

Audio Books

Mine, Body and Soul, Part One: The Playroom Series

Mine, Body and Soul, Part Two: The Playroom Series

Mine, Body and Soul, Part Three: The Playroom Series

Daddy Kink: The App (book one)

Always More: The Flamingo Bar (book one)

When Fake Changed Everything

Ferron's Journey: Damaged Part One

Ferron's Journey: Hidden Part Two

Ferron's Journey: Revelation Part Three

Romance books in a mixed series of M/F and M/M by the Author under a different pen name Jayne Paton

Smith's Corner

Delilah & Dallas (book one)

Layla & Levi (Book two)

Ash & Alora (Book three)

Fox & Faith (book four)

Storm & Stone (book five)

Hunter & Holden (book six)

Crime and Thrillers by the Author under a different pen name J Paton

Headspace
Chozen: Dark MM Crime Drama (Headspace Book 1)
Chozen: Dark MM Crime Drama (Headspace Book 2)

About the Author

Eccentric cake lover who has a passion for words of all kinds. I'm Jayne or JP, I live in the Isle of Man. A tiny place in the Irish sea where all the magic happens. I'm a confessed bookaholic and if I'm not writing I love to snuggle with a book or two...if you catch my drift.

If you're interested in keeping up to date, then I've a few places you can do that, and they're listed below. My website is where you'll find all the different Me's there are, LOL. As I travel this path into the future, I'm going to be writing in different genres so to stop there being any confusion I'll be writing under different pen names.

If you would like to give me any feedback or just have any questions, go ahead and friend me on Facebook, and I would be happy to answer anything. I hope you enjoyed this book and if you would also like to leave a review, then I would love to read your thoughts. Even if you just want to rate it, I'll be grateful

Thank you for being a part of my dream.

Newsletter Sign up
Goodreads
Tumblr
Bookbub
Instagram
Twitter
Facebook
Website address
Facebook Author page
JP Manx Minx's
Patreon